THE SECRETS BEHIND THE DOORWAY

MOHAMMED MUSTHAFA

Made with ♥ on the Notion Press Platform
www.notionpress.com

To my beloved family, KE Usman, Hyrunissa Usman, Nousheena, and Zaiha, whose unwavering love, support, and understanding have been my pillars of strength throughout this creative journey. Your presence in my life fuels my inspiration every day.

I also dedicate this book to my forensic mentor, Dr. Ravikanth Soni, whose guidance and knowledge have shaped not only my understanding of forensic science but also my passion for storytelling. Your wisdom and mentorship have been invaluable in bringing this novel to life.

Contents

Contents

Preface

In the tranquil landscapes of Kerala, where the whispers of coconut palms and the scent of spices fill the air, a tale unfolds. A tale woven through the narrative lens of Dr. Arnab, one that will take you on a journey through the intricacies of the human psyche, amidst a backdrop of crime and mystery.

Welcome to the world of psychological intrigue, where the boundaries between the mind's labyrinthine corridors and the tangible mysteries of the world blur. In this crime thriller, you will join Dr. Arnab in his relentless pursuit of the truth, where the answers lie not only in evidence but also in the recesses of the human mind.

As you delve into the pages of this narrative, you may encounter a sprinkle of Malayalam words, the essence of Kerala, where culture and crime intertwine. Fear not, for the essence of these words will enhance the authenticity of the story, bringing you closer to the vivid tapestry of this coastal state.

The time period in which this story unfolds is both familiar and unforgettable — the era before and after the tumultuous COVID-19 lockdown, spanning from 2020 to 2023. The pandemic has left indelible marks on our lives, and as you read, you may find echoes of these experiences mirrored in the lives of the characters.

The inspiration for this tale was drawn from the pages of newspapers, from the social problems that haunt our world. It is a reflection of the chaos and darkness that sometimes hide behind the façade of tranquility. In these pages, we explore the resilience of the human spirit and the depths of the human psyche, all against the backdrop of a world forever altered by a global crisis.

Prepare to embark on a journey that will test your wits, challenge your perceptions, and lead you into the heart of psychological suspense. This is a story of mysteries waiting to be unraveled, secrets yearning to be exposed, and minds teetering on the brink of revelation.

CHAPTER ONE

Dr Arnab Baweja's Narration

On January 25, 2023, I received an invitation for an interview regarding the award I had received the previous month from the Society of Experimental Psychologists, the Howard Crosby Award for excellence in experimental psychology in the United States and Canada.

As is customary, when an Indian wins a significant prize, media coverage and social media posts abound. Consequently, even our society, which had not previously taken an interest in my life, began to acknowledge and honor me. Given that almost everyone desires recognition, I decided to participate in the interview. The organization that contacted me, Asianet Media, requested my presence at their studio by 8 a.m. I prepared myself, took my car keys, started the engine, and as soon as I woke up at 6 a.m., I used my phone to input the location of "Asianet Studio" into my "Google Maps" navigation app. I arrived at the studio by 7:45 a.m. A woman sporting Wayfarer spectacles approached me. She was holding a clipboard and several papers.

"Mr. Arnab Baweja?"

"Dr. Arnab Baweja, the psychologist," I responded.

"Alright, Dr. Please come with me."

I followed her into the studio. My initial impression was one of surprise, as the studio exterior appeared disorderly. I wondered if this was the same location where I used to watch TV shows on television. However, inside, it was illuminated by numerous lights and cameras. The stage was immaculate, with two seats arranged. I continued following her until we reached the makeup room.

"Please wait here, Dr.," the lady instructed.

"When will the interview commence?" I inquired.

"The interviewer hasn't arrived yet. It might take around half an hour for her to reach here."

"Half an hour?" I was taken aback. "Wasn't the interview supposed to begin at 8 o'clock?"

"Yes, sir. I apologize for any inconvenience. The program will start as soon as the interviewer arrives. Please wait here."

"Very well," I acquiesced. "If you don't mind my asking, who will be conducting my interview?"

"Miss Meera Agarwal, sir."

"The lady with the..." I paused.

She smiled wryly and responded, "Yes, sir."

"Perfect," I remarked.

So, I waited there for an hour. The experience was akin to visiting a government office where lengthy waiting times are the norm for obtaining essential documents or Aadhaar cards. It's a common understanding that individuals like us receive less priority from society compared to politicians or movie stars.

Two hours later, I drifted off to sleep. I was eventually awakened by the woman wearing Wayfarer spectacles.

"Sir, hurry up! The interview is about to start. Please come quickly," she urged.

"Oh! Has she arrived?" I mumbled sleepily.

"Yes, sir. Please hurry."

My attire and hair were disheveled, so I quickly made myself presentable. Afterward, I followed her. Once I was on stage, Miss Agarwal, the interviewer, set up her omnidirectional microphone. Unfamiliar individuals tended to my makeup and attached the microphone to my collar. The director of the show began giving orders, and the crew members scurried behind the cameras.

"Is everything set with the lights? And the sound system?" the director inquired.

"All set, sir," a team member confirmed.

"Alright, then... ROLL SOUND... CAMERA... ACTION!"

The lights focused on me and Miss Agarwal.

"Hello and namaskar, everyone. This is Meera welcoming you to a very special episode of 'The Nobel Show.' Why is this episode special, you ask? Because we have with us Dr. Arnab Baweja, the recipient of the Howard Crosby Prize from the Society for Experimental Psychology, awarded for outstanding achievements in experimental psychology in the United States and Canada. Dr. Arnab, welcome to our show."

The audience applauded, and the interview began.

"Doctor, how do you feel about being an award-winning psychologist?" Meera inquired.

"To be honest, my primary aim wasn't solely to win awards," I explained. "My life has been dedicated to a deep-seated affection, preference, and passion for acquiring knowledge about human psychology."

"Really? But surely you must take pride in your awards?"

"In my case, the awards are a result of my opportunity to delve into my knowledge, to share my findings, and for that, I have been honored. It has brought me recognition, but I don't consider myself a fully accomplished individual. There's still much more I want to explore in the realm of human psychology. So, let's remain hopeful."

"You're being quite modest, I must say."

"It's not about modesty. The idea is that true success isn't just about awards or accolades. It's a journey of continuous learning and growth. Speaking of which, how many of you are familiar with the famous actor Salman Khan?"

The audience responded enthusiastically.

"Is he a successful person?" I questioned.

"Yes, he certainly is," Meera replied, a touch hesitantly.

"But did you know that there was a phase in his life when he faced financial difficulties and wasn't getting film offers, despite his fame? Anyone?"

The audience was taken aback and puzzled.

"Yes, it's true. However, now he's doing exceedingly well, with several movies entering the 100-crore club."

"Are you implying that you aren't successful?"

"Success isn't a fixed destination. It's an ongoing journey. As Winston Churchill said, 'Success is not final, failure is not fatal, it's the courage to continue that counts.' It's about the process and the progress."

The audience applauded my response.

"So, Doctor, what is your ultimate objective in this profession you've chosen?" Meera inquired further.

"As I mentioned earlier, my aim is to delve deeper into human psychology, understanding various emotions, different types of delusions, and so on."

"Different types of delusional mentalities? Why bring up that topic?"

"We all, in some way, possess certain delusions."

"Wait, are you saying we're all a bit crazy?" Meera teased, eliciting laughter from the audience.

"Do you believe you're entirely normal?" I asked, light-heartedly.

"Excuse me?" Meera responded, slightly taken aback.

"I'm sorry if that's a surprising question, but do you genuinely think you're a flawless individual?"

"Why are you asking that?"

"Because it's worth contemplating."

"Well... I suppose."

"In that case, let me ask you this: Is money the most powerful force in the world?"

"Of course, money is essential for survival."

"Congratulations, Meera. You're delusional," I replied, using a touch of sarcasm.

"What?" she exclaimed.

"MONEY is a universal illusion that makes us believe it's the sole means of survival. But the truth is, a billionaire can perish in a car accident."

"So, you're saying money is just paper?"

"From a logical standpoint, yes. But from a societal perspective, it's more than that."

"Uh-huh... I'm not sure what to make of that," Meera admitted.

"MONEY is a myth that compels us to think it's indispensable for survival. Yet, consider this: Brendon Grimshaw."

"Who's Brendon Grimshaw?"

"When Brendon Grimshaw worked at a London print shop, he led an unhappy life. People saw him as peculiar. He struggled to discern the true meaning of his existence. Can you imagine someone leading a seemingly stable life yet feeling dissatisfied?"

Meera's curiosity was piqued. "Go on."

"Well, he grew tired of his monotonous routine, the cycle of receiving a monthly income, covering rent, food, and other expenses, only to see his earnings dwindle by the end of the month. So, he took a bold step. He spent his entire savings, around $13,000, to purchase an island named 'Moyenne.'"

"Wow."

"Yes, he did. He left behind his old life and embarked on a new path. He began constructing a wooden house, befriended creatures like birds and turtles, and transformed the island into a paradise. Over time, he gained attention as 'THE MAN WHO BOUGHT A TROPICAL ISLAND AND TRANSFORMED IT.' People were curious about his lifestyle: 'How did he feed himself?' 'How did he live without the internet and cell phones?' 'How did he survive without money?' These were the questions on everyone's lips. But Brendon remained unfazed. In 2010, a Saudi prince offered him $50 million for the island, but Brendon turned down the offer. THE MAN WHO LIVED WITHOUT MONEY TURNED AN ISLAND INTO HEAVEN. In an interview years ago, he was asked if he ever felt lonely. His response was intriguing: 'Yes, I did feel lonely when I worked as an editor.' Fascinating, isn't it? He lived life on his terms, devoid of struggle, animosity, gossip, internet, or stress—simply living in peace."

The audience listened intently.

"It's quite a captivating life he led. So, believing in the notion that 'MONEY IS EVERYTHING' is a form of psychological delusion," Meera confessed emotionally.

"Indeed, Meera. Moreover, there's no unanimous consensus on the definition of 'abnormality or disorder.' It's a challenging concept to define definitively."

"Then what is your perspective on abnormal psychology?"

"I view a person as abnormal when their actions, as perceived by others, deviate significantly from what is expected and predictable in a given context."

Meera was intrigued. "Could you elaborate?"

"Consider this scenario: If a person next to you suddenly began shouting obscenities, you'd likely consider it abnormal behavior, right?"

"Um, yes, I suppose."

"That's because it's unpredictable and out of the ordinary. Yet, from that person's perspective, they're not acting abnormally, especially if they're experiencing a surge of joy."

"Interesting. Any specific aspects of abnormal psychology that captivate your interest?"

"I'm particularly drawn to criminal psychology," I confessed.

"Why criminal psychology?"

"Let me ask you this: Is stealing a packet of chips from a grocery store a criminal act?"

"Yes, certainly."

"But what if the person stealing the chips hadn't eaten in two days due to extreme hunger? A starving individual's ability to differentiate between right and wrong is compromised. Their primary focus is to feed themselves at any cost, 'JUST FEED' echoing in their mind. So, does this make them a criminal?"

"I'm not entirely sure."

"Exactly. Criminal psychology delves into these complexities. However, I'm not here to justify criminal acts. My goal is to understand the underlying causes that lead individuals down the path of lawlessness. There are individuals who suffer from antisocial personality disorder, such as impostors and contract killers. Both may display abnormal behavior, but from their perspective, it's a means of survival. Society sees it as deviant behavior, and while I'm not condoning it, there are segments that unintentionally rationalize it."

"I see your point. But what about more heinous criminals like murderers or rapists? How do they fit into your perspective?"

"I'm not the ultimate judge who passes sentence. My role is to unearth the factors that trigger such actions. Take, for example, Sukumara Kurup."

"Yes, the infamous criminal from Kerala. Everyone's familiar with his case."

"Indeed. There have been cinematic adaptations of his life, including one by Dulquer Salman."

The audience showed enthusiasm at the mention of Dulquer Salman.

"Exactly, but while these films never condone his horrific crime, their presentation varies. In an older film, the villain is captured by the police in the final scene, which resonated well with the audience at that time. However, in a newer adaptation, when the police claim to have captured Kurup, the audience response is different—almost disappointed. It's when a post-credits scene suggests Kurup's survival that the audience reacts ecstatically, despite knowing the gravity of his actions."

"Perhaps it's due to Dulquer's fan base?" Meera suggested.

"Of course, but that doesn't validate the character's actions."

"True."

"Consider this: people are often more drawn to how a particular scenario is portrayed. Just as I mentioned with the example of the starving man who stole food to feed himself – from his perspective, this is a 'representation'; his action was driven by necessity. Then there's Kurup, the man who committed a crime for insurance money. Each scenario has its own unique way of being portrayed. People encode these representations into their subconscious minds, influencing their actions without their conscious awareness. They navigate paths they may not even be aware of, some of which might not be the right ones. To elaborate, think of a person who uses cocaine; gradually, they become addicted to it, making it difficult for them to break free. The same principle applies here. My vision is to delve into the underlying causes, to find a way to liberate them from these influences – what we doctors refer to as 'treatment.'"

"I'm truly honored. I sincerely hope that one day you'll achieve your goal, Doctor."

"Thank you very much. Your words mean a lot to me," I responded with genuine happiness.

"Thank you, Doctor. It was an excellent interview." Meera turned towards the audience.

"Until we meet again next week on 'The Nobel Show,' this is Meera Agarwal bidding farewell."

Applause filled the room. The director called out "CUT," signaling the end of the show, and the lights were dimmed. "Wonderful interview. It was a pleasure to meet you, Doctor."

"Thank you," I replied warmly.

"I look forward to our paths crossing again. Goodbye." Meera waved as she exited with her team. The set was disassembled, and I returned to my home.

A few days later, I visited my clinic as usual and engaged with a range of patients, including those struggling with depression and mood swings. Each day followed the same routine.

After my counseling session, a well-known Punjabi businessman who was battling work-related depression left the clinic. Just as he exited, a teenage girl with frizzy hair and an asymmetrical dress entered. She gave the Punjabi man a look that I instantly recognized.

"Please come in and have a seat," I invited her.

She entered and took a chair. I began to observe her nonverbal cues, deducing from her behavior that she was bewildered due to a recent chaotic event in her life.

"Is he the person who started his own building steel company in India?" The lady inquired, referring to the businessman she had just seen in a magazine five days ago.

"Remarkable that you recognized him from a picture in an article, even though you only saw it recently. You have an excellent memory," I remarked.

She managed a smile, though her demeanor still held a touch of sadness. To establish a rapport, I introduced myself.

"Hello, I'm Dr. Arnab Baweja," I introduced.

"Ankhitha Murali," she responded with her own introduction.

"A lovely name. So, how can I assist you?" I inquired.

"Hmm... I'm not entirely sure about this..." she hesitated.

"Pardon me?" I asked, curious.

"I think I should leave," she stood up, displaying signs of anxiety.

"Ah, please don't go," I implored. "If you leave abruptly, those waiting outside might think I'm an inexperienced doctor, potentially damaging my reputation. I kindly ask you to stay a bit longer before leaving."

This approach was meant to evoke a sense of regret in her for leaving and to keep her in the room for a few more minutes. She remained seated, her hands resting on her thighs – a telltale sign that she was trying to wipe her sweaty palms. These actions hinted at her stress.

To alleviate her discomfort and encourage her to open up, I decided to share a story. I conjured up a tale in an instant.

"Once upon a time, there was a man who spent most of his life aboard a ship, sailing across oceans," I began. "One morning, at around 7 o'clock, he was quietly listening to the sounds of the sea when something caught his attention in the distance. It was a green, luminous flash. He fetched his binoculars to get a closer look and was utterly astounded."

"What did he see?" the lady asked, her curiosity piqued.

"He saw a ship not sailing atop the sea, but floating through the air. Yes, the ship was flying."

"How is that even possible?"

"It may sound unbelievable, but yes – it's a true story, it really happened."

"How?"

"What are your thoughts?"

"There must be a reason, a legitimate scientific explanation."

"Indeed, there was one. However, I won't reveal it until you share the reason you're here."

"Oh, if I tell you, you might think I'm crazy."

"Is my story any more logical?"

"Heh, not really."

"But regardless, it's true. Now, please tell me what's troubling you?"

She leaned forward slightly, her hands trembling and her lips quivering. After a moment, she began to speak,

"Dr. Arnab... I believe I witnessed a murder."

CHAPTER TWO

Ankitha Speaks

We are residents of Skyline Flat in Thrissur, comprising Block A and Block B. My apartment was situated on the seventh floor of Block A. The two buildings were positioned side by side. On July 19, 2020, which happened to be my 20th birthday, I reached out to some of my neighbors and friends who also called this apartment complex home. Due to the Covid-19 lockdown protocols, I couldn't extend invitations to a few friends residing beyond our apartment premises. Consequently, we organized a Zoom video conference for them, using a projector to display the call on the wall.

At noon, everyone gathered, and the cake was carefully placed on the table. As the melodious tune of the birthday song filled the air, my friend Basi mischievously decided to adorn my face with a smudge of cake cream.

In an outburst of frustration, I exclaimed, "What on earth are you up to? You've completely ruined my makeup! Seriously, what's wrong with you, you idiot?"

Basi, with a hint of sarcasm, fired back, "Well, now everyone gets to see your true, unadorned face." In response, I swiftly retorted, "Oh, just go to hell."

The atmosphere instantly lightened as everyone began playfully bantering, snapping pictures of me to share on Instagram, and even crafting light-hearted memes. Despite the good-natured intent, I couldn't shake off the sense of humiliation that settled within me.

After a while, everyone began interacting with each other while eating. I went in search of my friend Greeshma, and as I had anticipated, I found her sitting alone in the corner, devouring four shawarmas. Her constant obsession with food is understandable, considering how she has gained weight over time. I approached her with a couple of shawarma wraps in hand and handed them to her.

Insisting, I said, "Give them a try. I made these."

"Sure, let me taste them." She eagerly took the wraps, biting into them as though she hadn't eaten in a decade.

"Mmmmm... these taste amazing, as always. Your culinary skills are unmatched. Your future spouse is lucky to have such a skilled cook," Greeshma remarked teasingly.

"Oh, come on!" I argued, "I didn't learn to cook just to feed my future spouse. I'm trying to finish my BCom course as quickly as possible so that I can enroll in a culinary program. Unfortunately, these unfortunate circumstances are delaying all my plans. The exams keep getting postponed, and I'm fed up with all of this."

"Dude... people might start calling you a cook," she quipped.

"I couldn't care less. Only dimwits like you would call me that."

"Are your parents going to be okay with this?"

"They haven't been so far, but eventually they will be."

Greeshma grinned just as the electricity suddenly went out.

"Like always, the power goes off, right at 8 PM and 12 AM," I remarked as the power came back on after a short while.

"Thanks a lot, KSEB," I said sarcastically.

In the early hours of the morning, my close friends Basi and Greeshma stayed by my side, while some of our companions left the party at 1:30 a.m. Greeshma's mother called frantically, inquiring about her whereabouts and urging her to return immediately, as it was already 1:30 a.m.

Greeshma reassured her, "Relax, Mom. I'm on my way."

Every time a girl spends the night somewhere else, the typical Indian mother becomes restless.

In our quest to reach the elevator, Basi, Greeshma, and I made our way. Gouri Prakash, our next-door neighbor, trailed behind us, casting a perplexed look in our direction. She wore a maroon sari and sported a large, round red dot on her forehead. Gouri was known for concocting and spreading false rumors, earning her disdain from all of us. Irritation and resentment had taken root due to her actions. To playfully provoke her, I deliberately rested my hand on Basi's shoulder.

"Basi ... my new beau," I remarked.

Gowri let out a derisive snort before heading towards the elevator. Basi appeared taken aback by my gesture; I could practically hear his heart racing, and a faint sheen of sweat formed on his brow. Girls had never before introduced him as their boyfriend.

"Take care," I added with a mischievous grin.

Basi appeared slightly flustered as he walked towards the closing sliding doors of the elevator. Greeshma broke into laughter as the doors shut.

"That meddler will undoubtedly twist the story in her own unique way. She's more treacherous than the coronavirus," Greeshma remarked, a blend of sarcasm and genuine concern in her tone.

"Let her try ... the whole world is well aware of her character. No one will lend her any credibility," I responded.

"You're truly something else, you know that?"

"Yes, I admit it. I'm feeling a bit like a troublemaker."

"Whatever," Greeshma retorted, a mix of irritation and amusement dancing in her eyes.

With that, Greeshma stepped into the elevator and it carried her away.

The clock read 2:00 AM, and I found myself in my room, engrossed in an episode of "Stranger Things" on Netflix while reclining on my bed. The sudden appearance of a spooky scene startled me, prompting me to pause and leave for the dining hall.

I took a sip of water before returning to my room and settling back onto the bed. I felt uneasy due to the light from the window continuously shining on my face. I moved to the window to draw the curtains, only to witness a puzzling sight from the neighboring flat's window. It seemed like someone was in the act of strangling another person. The scene was unclear, driving me to frantically search for my binoculars around the room. Once found, I peered through the binoculars placed on my study table, revealing a woman wielding an object like a rod to viciously strike a man's head.

Panic surged through me, causing my binoculars to slip from my grasp as fear gripped me. I cried out and rushed into my father's bedroom.

"Daddy, wake up, Dad!" I called urgently.

Startled, my father asked, "Why are you screaming? What's wrong?"

In a frightened plea, I told my Dad, "Dad, I witnessed a murder. Please call the police."

"A murder? Where?" he inquired.

"I saw a woman attacking someone in Block B, Dad," I implored him to take action.

"Hold on, let me contact security first," my father said as he got up and headed to the main hall. He picked up the service phone and made a call to security.

The security officer on the other end answered with a yawn.

"Meet me at Block B immediately. I'm already on my way," my father instructed.

"What's going on, sir? It's late," the security officer questioned.

Frustrated, my father's voice grew sharper. "Just do as I say."

With my mother and father beside me, we hurried to the elevator, descended to the ground floor, and swiftly headed towards Block B. A guard was stationed there, waiting.

I addressed the security guard, urgency in my voice, "Please come with us to the seventh floor, and please hurry."

"Wait, ma'am—what's happening?" the guard asked.

"Please come; there's no time to explain."

The security guards guided us to the elevator, and we entered, pressing the button for the seventh floor. Emotions surged as the elevator seemed to take an eternity to reach its destination. Finally, we arrived. Amidst my heightened emotions, I struggled to identify which of the three apartments on the seventh floor was the scene of the murder. I rang the doorbells of all three apartments: 7-A, 7-B, and 7-C. Only the occupants of 7-A and 7-B answered, both in an unpleasant manner, while there was no response from 7-C.

Pointing to the occupants of 7-A and 7-B, I explained, "I believe it was one of these apartments. Dad, please call the police."

"Murder?" the security officer echoed, taken aback.

"Yes, could you please unlock the door?" I urgently requested.

"Ma'am, this apartment has been vacant for the past two years. It was recently rented by a bachelor," the security guard revealed.

My father asked, "Whose apartment is this?"

"Sir, it belongs to an NRI residing in Dubai who purchased this property."

Imploringly, I turned to my father. "Dad, you have to believe me. I saw the murder happen, and the victim might still be alive. Please do something."

"Is there a spare key available?" my father inquired of the security officer.

"Yes, sir," the security guard replied.

"Retrieve it. Let's unlock the door."

"But, Sir..."

"Go ahead. Don't worry; I'll take responsibility if anything goes wrong."

"Alright, sir," the security guard acquiesced, making his way to the elevator. As I knocked and rang the doorbell persistently, I noticed curious stares from onlookers. My sole focus was on ensuring the well-being of the individual I had seen. Finally, the door opened, revealing a person with curly hair, a weary expression, dressed in a black t-shirt and shorts. To my astonishment, this person was not the same man I had witnessed being attacked by the woman. Stepping into the apartment,Upon entering, I noticed a large mirror positioned close to the balcony. I urgently exclaimed, "There's been a murder! I saw it from my window over there," pointing to the balcony.

Glancing out from the balcony, I could see my own apartment. I hurriedly took my father to the balcony, showing him, "Dad, look, that's my room window. I saw everything from there. We can see our apartment from here."

"Was it a nightmare or did you genuinely witness this?" my mother asked cautiously.

Frustrated, I retorted, "Mom, please, I really saw it."

"You're awake all night watching movies on your phone, that's why," my mother countered.

Addressing my mother by name, my father intervened, "Gayathry, let's not argue about that now."

"Just saying," my mother muttered.

Confused, the occupant of the apartment asked, "What's happening? Why are you bothering me so late?"

I proceeded to search every room, bathroom, and kitchen like a mad person, desperately seeking any sign of the victim's body. Yet, my search yielded no results.

"Molee, it might have been a dream," my mother suggested.

"No!" I exclaimed, my determination evident. "I'm certain I saw it." I turned to my father, my eyes pleading for his belief. In his reassuring embrace, I found some comfort, even as others in the crowd began to see me as irrational. Amidst my mumblings about having witnessed a crime, we returned to our apartment.

CHAPTER THREE

After witnessing the murder, when we returned to our apartment, the fear was too overwhelming for me to sleep alone, especially in my room. So, that night, I slept with my parents. I was torn between feelings of remorse, anxiety, and fear, which made falling asleep a struggle. The next day, I waited for the police to arrive to collect the body and take my statement. However, nothing happened. When I went downstairs, I noticed everyone was giving me strange looks. I couldn't help but keep staring at Block B on the seventh floor, as if I was drawn to it. Greeshma's sudden jolt brought me back to reality.

"What's going on, Ankitha? What happened last night? People are talking about you," Greeshma inquired curiously.

"I'm completely confused right now. I expected the police to come here and investigate the murder I witnessed last night, but nothing has happened," I said in a disorganized and impatient manner.

"What murder? Ankitha, are you even listening to yourself?" Greeshma responded.

"I saw it there, Greeshma, I'm certain of that. In Block B," I pointed towards the seventh floor window.

"Remember the show you watched last night? What was it called?" Greeshma suggested.

"It has nothing to do with the series 'Stranger Things,'" I replied.

"Well, it might just be a dream, you know," Greeshma said.

"But, Greeshma, I can tell the difference between a dream and reality."

"Okay, relax."

"I think we should call the police."

"Are you out of your mind? That might create more problems."

"So, what do I do now?"

"You should stop talking about this. Otherwise, people might start thinking you're losing it."

"I don't understand why nobody believes me."

"Ankitha, because it doesn't make sense."

"Leave me alone!" I shouted at her, retreating back to the entrance of Block A.

"Ankitha, wait," Greeshma hurriedly followed me.

Inside the elevator, I pressed the close button, trying to keep Greeshma out. As I entered my apartment, I grabbed my phone and sat down on the couch. Suddenly, my mother grabbed my phone.

"Your constant use of this thing is giving you these nightmares and embarrassing both your father and me," my mother scolded.

"Please give it back, don't make a scene."

"Am I the one causing trouble? I won't give it to you."

"Mom, what's gotten into you?"

"Do you even know what you did last night?"

"Mom, I know exactly what I did. Anyone would react the same way if they witnessed a murder."

"Foolish girl, why do you keep clinging to this? Are you insane?"

"Please, Mom, give me my phone."

"No, I won't."

"Don't be ridiculous, Mom. Just give it to me."

"You called me ridiculous? How dare you?" My mother's anger flared as she threw my phone to the ground, shattering it into pieces.

"Mom, what the hell?" I exclaimed.

Hearing the commotion, my father entered the room. I sobbed and left the living room for the hallway, where I stayed alone, crying. Am I really crazy? I began to question myself. Was the crime all in my head? These thoughts overwhelmed me, causing me to overthink. After a while, my father joined me, sitting behind me. He handed me a tissue as I wiped my tears.

"Dad, am I truly going crazy?" I sobbed, my tears flowing freely.

"Don't say that. You're one of the bravest girls I know," he reassured me.

"Don't lie, Dad."

"I'm not lying. Most people would have run away when faced with witnessing a murder, but your instinct was to save that person. If people think that's crazy, then the world, not you, is crazy."

"So, you believe me, right?" I immediately asked.

"Sometimes, nightmares can feel very real, Mole."

"But, Dad, I'm sure I saw it. It wasn't like a dream."

"Mole, there are moments when it's hard to distinguish between a dream and reality."

"So, you don't believe me either." I snapped. "Please leave, Dad. I need to be alone."

"Molee, I do believe you," he intentionally fibbed to provide comfort.

"Dad, please go."

My father got up and left the room. I felt guilty for not saving that person, and I couldn't tell if I had really witnessed the murder or not. These thoughts left me feeling incredibly isolated. The more I tried to convince people that I saw the murder, the less they seemed to believe me. Gradually, the idea that I might truly be crazy started to take hold.

TWO DAYS LATER

I sat alone at a playground, feeling uneasy and isolated. Greeshma joined me, bringing her usual two shawarmas. She handed one to me.

"Have it while it's hot," she suggested.

"I'm not really in the mood for a shawarma right now," I replied.

"It's hot, flavorful, and delicious."

"I said no."

"If you say so, don't complain later that I didn't share."

"I'm not a compulsive food lover like you," I teased.

"Fine then..." Greeshma replied, taking a big bite in front of me, which didn't bother me at all. As Gowri Prakash walked by, Greeshma commented cynically, "Here comes Gowri, tang tang

tang!"

I laughed uncontrollably at that. Gowri glanced our way briefly before moving in our direction.

"Oh great, why is she coming over?" I muttered.

"Maybe she's got a fresh piece of gossip to spread," Greeshma quipped, "Let her come."

Gowri approached with a smile. "Hey there, how are you, Mole?"

"I'm alright, aunty," I replied.

"I heard you've been dealing with some mental issues. Is everything getting better?" Gowri asked.

Her words hit me hard, and I felt tears welling up. I got up and walked away. Greeshma shot Gowri a glare.

"She is much better than you, madwoman," Greeshma said as she walked up to me and took my hand.

"It's disheartening that people have started treating me like a lunatic," I replied with a pained tone.

"Ankhitha, are you really taking what she said seriously? Ignore her; she's unstable," Greeshma responded.

"Still..."

"Enough of that. Let's go to Basi's home and confront him."

"I forgot, where was he during all of this?"

"So he didn't tell you?"

"Tell me what?"

"Yes, he didn't inform me either; he went to Kochi."

"Why?"

"There's a reason behind it. What's the reason?"

"He's been in touch with a girl for a while; he has a crush on her."

"Yes, Vaishnavi, I had a suspicion."

"Yes, she agreed when he invited her to go with him."

"Really?" I was astonished. "Then we must go see him immediately."

Greeshma and I arrived at his flat and rang the doorbell. Basi's mother swung the door open.

"Hello, aunty," Greeshma greeted.

"Hey kids, how are you two?" Basi's mother inquired.

"We're good, aunty," Greeshma replied, sympathizing with me. Basi's mother turned to me.

"And how about you, Ankhitha dear?"

"I'm fine, aunty," I replied, feeling her compassionate gaze. Greeshma then inquired directly.

"Where's Basi, aunty?"

"He's in his room."

"Let's go see him."

We entered his room. Basi sat on the bed with a forlorn expression. We walked over and settled on the bed beside him.

"How was your day, bro? Enjoyed yourself with Vaishnavi?" Greeshma asked.

Looking at me, he let out a sorrowful sigh.

"Bro, why the gloomy face?" I asked.

"Did Vaishnavi stand you up?" Greeshma joked. I burst into laughter.

Emotionally, Basi confessed, "I think I'm destined to remain single."

"Why?" I asked. "Didn't you have a date with Vaishnavi?"

Regrettably, Basi responded, "She didn't show up."

"Why, brother?" Greeshma queried, a soft chuckle escaping her lips.

Basi shot Greeshma an intense glare.

"I'm sorry. Please tell us what happened," Greeshma urged.

"I had so many plans for her: a candlelit dinner, watching 'Kuch Kuch Hota Hai' while cuddling. Everything fell apart," Basi sadly recounted.

"How many times have you seen 'Dostana'?" I playfully interjected.

"Enough, let him finish," Greeshma scolded me.

"Go on, bro, what happened?" I asked.

"I reached Kochi Bus station. I waited there for an hour, imagining lovely moments with her," Basi said.

"And then?" I prompted.

"I got a call from Vaishnavi. She said she couldn't come because her parents were being strict due to the pandemic. She hung up after that. But her WhatsApp status showed her with a guy who had six-pack abs. She lied to me," Basi revealed.

Greeshma and I exchanged glances, laughing heartily.

"So, what did you do in Kochi these last two days?" I inquired.

"I wandered around, spent time at LuLu Mall and Marine Drive," Basi claimed.

"Come on, man, let her go. You'll find someone better," Greeshma advised. "Just be patient, bro."

Basi retorted angrily, "I've heard that a million times."

"Okay, calm down," Greeshma soothed.

"Whatever. Hey Ankhitha, why does everyone say you've gone crazy since I got here?" Basi asked.

"Long story, bro," Greeshma replied.

Basi questioned, "What happened here?"

Greeshma explained, "Well, Ankhitha claims she witnessed a murder."

"Who got killed?" Basi exclaimed.

"No one. Stop shouting," Greeshma reassured him.

"I saw the crime. It's true. Whether you believe it or not, I'll get to the bottom of this," I said, my anger evident.

"Relax, Ankhitha," Greeshma said.

"No wonder my mom warned me against talking to Ankitha," Basi mused, turning to face me.

Greeshma softly slapped Basi, whispering "Shhh" to him. Hearing that left me feeling melancholic. I stood up and walked out.

"Hey Ankhitha, come here," Greeshma called, but I ignored her.

"What's wrong with you, Basi?" Greeshma questioned.

"I said it without thinking. I apologize," Basi said.

"Idiot," Greeshma muttered.

Back home, I couldn't hold back my tears. My Dad came to me, hugged me, and suggested, "Let's visit grandma at home, spend some time there."

"Dad, that's risky. She's old; Corona could be dangerous for her," I hesitated.

"If the RTPCR results are negative, we can consider it."

"But the local authorities might not allow us to leave the neighborhood."

"It's not as strict as before. We can leave now."

"Oh right, I forgot Basi just returned from Kochi," I said, realizing it might be best to leave for a while.

So we all made the decision to visit our ancestral home. More than my parents, my grandmother will understand how I feel.

CHAPTER FOUR

27TH MARCH 2023

After three years, I found myself returning to my previous way of life. I had successfully completed the BCOM course. Despite the lockdowns and the containment of the Corona pandemic, occasional reports of COVID cases still reached us. Our residence remained the same, the Skyline apartment, yet my room, which had been the window through which I witnessed the murder, had remained locked for three years; we hadn't set foot in it. The fear from that day still haunted me, but over time, we all began to push it further from our minds.

I embarked on a quest to find a reputable university, diligently scouring websites, Instagram profiles, and newspapers to locate a suitable culinary course to enroll in. Gradually, my dad's initial unease gave way to acceptance, though my mom remained resistant. At 23 years old, my mother was eager for me to get married as soon as possible. A conflict had emerged between us, and we had been arguing about it for a while.

On one occasion, as our family gathered in the main hall, my mom turned to my dad and said, "Etta, our family friend Sharadha called me a little while ago."

Curious, Dad inquired, "What for?"

Looking at me, my mom continued, "She invited us to her daughter's engagement. The girl is only 22 and always respects her parents."

I pretended not to pay much attention.

"Well then, I suppose we should attend. When is it?" Dad asked.

"Next Friday."

Dad mused, "How fast our children are growing up."

In a somewhat condescending tone, Mom remarked, "Yes, her friend is getting engaged to a doctor, and here our daughter still hasn't grown out of her aspirations to become a hash slinger."

I corrected her, "It's a chef, Mom. That's the word."

With a playful smile, my dad glanced at me, which helped alleviate my frustration as I shot him an irritated look. In many Malayalee households, placing newspapers on the table before meals was a common practice, making it easy to roll up food waste and dispose of it. I stood up and gathered a few old newspapers that were lying in a corner. Taking a few sheets, I started arranging them on the dining table. While doing so, I stumbled upon a photograph in the newspaper that struck me as oddly familiar. Intrigued, I picked up the sheet and examined it closely. I couldn't shake off the feeling that I recognized that face. Yes, that was the man's face I had seen on my birthday three years ago, the same face that had met its end on the seventh level of block B. Startled, I rushed over to my father.

Pointing to the man's picture in the newspaper, I exclaimed, "Dad, he's the one, Dad."

My father looked at the photo. Mom emerged from the kitchen.

"What's going on? Why are you shouting, Ankhitha?" Mom asked.

I informed her, "Mom, this is the person who died that night."

Confused, Mom questioned, "Which night?"

"Remember the night I witnessed a murder on the seventh floor of B block three years ago?"

"Oh no, not again. Please let it go, Molee," Mom pleaded in a tense tone.

"Hey, take a look at the story," Dad intervened.

My father and I delved into the article.

"CHAIRMAN OF AL ZUBAIR BUILDING MATERIAL BUSINESS DIES IN SINGLE CAR ACCIDENT

Anwar Zubair, the head of Al Zubair Building Materials, passed away on July 20th after the Hyundai i20 he was driving collided with a tree in the Anaikatti area of Palakkad district. The collision occurred near the Attapadi Reserve Forest during the early hours of the morning. A fierce thunderstorm and heavy rainfall had swept through the region, uprooting trees and leaving the area without electricity for the night. He had checked in at the "Komaram Lodge" motel in Anakkatti at 6:00 a.m. on July 19th and left the following morning. A copy of his driver's license was retained as evidence of his stay at the lodge. The impact had claimed his life instantly. His body was found within the vehicle; the force of the impact had caused his head to collide with a large tree branch, resulting in upper body compression. His face was beyond recognition due to the crash. His family members identified the body based on his car's registration number, his once-worn Rolex watch, his attire, and the vehicle itself. A partially burnt driver's license was discovered in his wallet. This incident was one of several recent accidents along this stretch of the highway.

"Mole," Dad remarked, "according to the article, he died in a car accident."

The article was released on July 21, 2020, as per the newspaper I checked.

'Dad, I witnessed the crime on July 19th at 2 a.m.'," I recounted.

"Yeah, but it states 'July 19th at night,' and he was checked in at the motel too," Dad pointed to a line that read, "On July 19, at 6:00 AM, he arrived at the 'Komaram Lodge' motel in Anakkatti."

"I'm sure that this is the guy who was killed that night," I affirmed.

Dad told me, 'Molee, we managed to resolve this issue; don't dig it up.'"

"Don't let people call you crazy again," Mama advised me.

"As always, nobody believes me. I'm the only one who has carried the guilt in my heart for these three years, for not being able to save him that day," I said, walking out of the room.

"Molee, please!" Dad shouted.

I can't believe it. I've never seen this guy before, so how can I see him in my dreams? I am positive beyond a shadow of a doubt that I saw him being assaulted that night. How can I back it up? Honestly, I have no evidence. If it was murder, there must be a way to prove it.

My mom and I don't speak for a day after a fight. However, whenever I'm famished, I used to go to the kitchen in silence to prepare a meal. My mother always organized food and left it in the kitchen, knowing I would go there for a meal. That night, I repeated the same routine. While my parents were watching Dr. Arnab's interview on the Asianet channel, Dad called out to me.

"Come watch this; it's interesting," Dad said.

I ignored my mother, took the food, and sat down on the couch. I paid close attention to the interview. I had the feeling that Dr. Arnab was the only person who might believe my story. I searched for information about you and eventually found this place.

CHAPTER FIVE

Present day (Dr Arnab's Narration)

"So, Dr. Arnab, what do you think? Am I crazy?" Ankhitha questioned.

I chuckled, "Crazy? Do you think I'm normal?" I inquired.

"How can I say that? I'm not a doctor like you."

"Hehe, if that's the case, all the Skyline residents are medical professionals."

"Really? How?"

"Because after they confirmed that you're insane, you burst into tears."

Ankhitha looked down, a few tiny tears shimmering in her eyes.

"There are professionals who can analyze and report on it. It's not up to them to determine if you're crazy or not. I can assure you that you're not crazy."

She grinned, a hint of motivation dawning. "So, Dr. Arnab, you do believe me?"

"There are reasons to believe you, as well as reasons not to," I replied.

"I expected that, fine then. I'm leaving," Ankhitha said in an agitated tone.

"Hey, calm down; just give me a little time,"

"How much time?"

"Would you accept someone's proposal as soon as it's presented to you? No, you'd give it more thought and evaluate it."

"Good point, yes."

"You're so stubborn and impatient; you know that."

"Yes, that's part of my nature."

I added with a hint of playfulness, "That's actually quite charming." Ankhitha gave me an odd look.

"I meant to say, that's a quality you possess," I clarified.

"Can you help me uncover what happened on that day?" Ankhitha asked, a grin directed my way.

"I have no choice since you've asked for my assistance. I must do something."

"But how?"

"The events of that day occurred in your room, so I need to start by visiting your apartment."

Ankhitha exclaimed fearfully, "I'm so scared to go into that room."

"To solve this mystery, I need your help too, Ankhitha. You'll need to face your fear."

Ankhitha sighed. "All right, doctor. When are you coming?"

"I'll come after I finish my shift at 4 p.m. tomorrow, alright?" I asked.

"I'll wait for you, doctor."

"Share your location on WhatsApp. You'll get my phone number in the reception area."

"Okay," she said, then got up. "I have no one else; you're my last hope, doctor, to prove that I'm right."

I nodded, a grin still on my face. She walked out.

Finally, my workday came to an end at 4 p.m., leaving me sweaty, exhausted, and fatigued. I returned home and rang the doorbell. My mother opened the door in an irritated manner, engrossed in watching a TV serial. As I entered my room, I sank into the comfort of my bed. After a while, my younger sister Gayathry, a third-year medical student, returned home from her class. She has a habit of frequently borrowing my phone, and this time she took the liberty to explore Ankhitha's WhatsApp chat.

Ankhitha: "What time will you be at my place tomorrow, Arnab?"

she observed the WhatsApp conversation between Ankhitha and the accompanying Google Map pin location.

"Momma... Momma!" I jolted awake as Gayathry's voice pierced the air.

She hurried towards the dining hall, showing something on my phone to Amma. Startled by her sudden outburst, I hastily followed her.

Gayathry informed my mother, "Amma, Chettayi has a girlfriend."

Her words caught me off guard. "Wait, what are you talking about?"

Gayathry explained, "Amma, look at this. Chettayi only has WhatsApp groups in his conversation list, but there's one person he's privately messaging." She proceeded to select Ankhitha's WhatsApp profile picture.

"Who is this Monee? She looks so lovely," Amma inquired.

I quickly responded, "Oh, she's just a patient of mine, Amma."

"Amma, he's lying. Why is he only messaging this 'patient' and not the others?" Gayathry challenged.

I hastily took my phone back, retorting, "Because her case is unique."

"But seriously, she's so pretty. Is she married?" Amma questioned.

"Enough, Amma. She's just a patient, nothing more," I asserted.

"Mone, you're 32 now. You've done everything you wanted. It's time for you to settle down," Amma said with a touch of concern.

"Amma, please, not again," I responded, feeling annoyed.

"Even I want to see my grandkids while I'm alive. I won't say more," Amma muttered as she walked into the kitchen.

"Unique situation, huh?" Gayathry smirked, giving me an odd look.

I warned, "I'm going to get you," as I playfully grabbed her arm.

"Don't be a chicken. You never give your number to anyone," she pushed back. "Why only her?"

"Let's go to my room; I'll explain everything," I suggested.

In my room, I proceeded to recount Ankhitha's story in detail.

"Interesting story," Gayathry commented. "Sounds like something out of a horror movie."

"There's no such thing as horror," I dismissed.

"She was the only witness to the crime, though. How's that possible? And no one else noticed it either."

"She might not have seen anything, just imagined it."

"But, Chettayi, what if she actually saw something?"

"Possible but not likely. Everything contradicts her story."

"What could be her problem then?"

"This happened during the lockdown. Most people there were just lying in bed, watching movies on their phones all day. Physical activity is important to produce serotonin, a mood-regulating hormone. Lack of exercise can lead to fear, depression, and disrupted sleep. She was watching a lot of horror and crime shows on Netflix, and that could've planted false memories in her mind."

"But what about the guy's picture in the news article?"

"Also a false memory. We see many people every day, and our subconscious retains vague images of them. She fabricated an extreme scenario. She finds it hard to believe she made it up."

"So, how will you help her?"

"She's haunted by a false memory of witnessing the crime on level 7 of block B. I need to alleviate her fear first."

"Still quite a unique situation, huh?" Gayathry teased.

I groaned, "Please, not again."

"Come on, Chettayi. She's really attractive. Give it a shot."

"Just drop it, please."

"I wouldn't mind having a sister-in-law," Gayathry chuckled as she left the room.

Ducking, I threw a pillow after her. Grabbing my phone, I opened it, and Ankhitha's picture unexpectedly filled the screen.

"Indeed, she's beautiful," I murmured to myself before quickly switching to another app to change my mood.

CHAPTER SIX

I headed to the clinic at 8 a.m. as usual, only to find some therapy clients waiting when I arrived. During my lunch break, a WhatsApp message popped up. It was from Ankhitha.

Ankhitha: "Meeting today at four, right?"

Arnab: "Yes, :)"

Ankhitha: "Will you be there? :/"

Arnab: "Of course, Ankhitha. Can't you trust me?"

Ankhitha: "It's not that; every time I share my story, people just dismiss me as crazy."

Arnab: "Don't be so pessimistic, Ankhitha. I'll be there at 4 o'clock sharp. Don't worry."

After she sent me an adorable smiley sticker, I replied with a thumbs-up emoji. Ankhitha was truly charming and had a childlike innocence that I found endearing. My mother and Gayathry also thought highly of her. As I clicked on her profile picture, I began to contemplate whether to maintain a strictly professional doctor-patient relationship or take a step further and become friends. Despite being the recipient of the Howard Crosby Award for excellence in experimental psychology, I found myself in a perplexing situation regarding how to approach a woman I had a crush on. Well, it didn't matter. I simply put my phone away and returned to the clinic area.

During a lull in patient appointments, my thoughts gravitated towards Ankhitha and how I could convince her that her memory of witnessing a murder was false. Then, a notion struck me: if I disclosed the truth, she wouldn't believe me and might even become more entrenched in her belief. I could, however, gradually shift her perspective by feigning acceptance of her story. It would take time, but I believed it could work.

I walked to Block A's seventh level and rang the doorbell of 7B. An elderly woman, appearing to be around 40 to 45 years old, answered the door.

The woman asked, "Who are you?"

"Dr. Arnab. I am..." Just as I was about to speak, she interrupted me.

“Hello, I think I've seen you somewhere, but I'm not sure. Have we met before?”

I replied, "Not that I‘m aware of."

“Hey, I believe we first met at Shailaja's daughter's nuptials.”

“I have no idea who Shailaja is, I'm sorry, ma'am."

Ankhitha hurried over to us from one of the apartment's rooms.

"Mom, he's Dr. Arnab; we saw his interview on Asianet, remember?" Ankhitha said to her mother.

“What interview?” her mom inquired.

"Mom, he was talking about mental health issues, the Kurup story, and all that," Ankhitha said.

"Oooh yes! That mental specialist," her mother said, surprising me in a humorous way.

Ankhitha apologetically remarked, "Psychologist, Mom."

My mother questioned, "Why is he here?"

Ankhitha responded, "I called him, Mom."

Her mother pulled Ankhitha into a corner, wearing an uneasy expression.

“Why did you bring him here?” Ankhitha's mother spoke to her in a hushed tone.

"I told him about that event and how I perceived the murder."

"Now you want to publicly display your insanity."

"I need to prove that I was right that day."

"Ankhitha, are you listening to yourself? This man could destroy you and your reputation. You won't find a spouse."

"I'm not bothered." Ankhitha walked over to me and said, "Come in, Dr. Arnab."

I entered and took a seat on the couch.

"What would you like, Doctor? Coffee or tea?" Ankhitha asked.

"I'll take some poisonous water, please," I said sarcastically, making Ankhita glare angrily at her mother before heading to the kitchen. I restrained my laughter as her mother shot me a furious look. I noticed the strained connection between the mother and daughter. When her father emerged from his office, he gave me a strange look.

I stood up and extended my hand, saying, "Hello, sir, I am Dr. Arnab."

Shaking my hand, he said, "Hi, I'm Murali; have we met before? You seem so familiar."

"You may have recently seen my interview," I said.

Ankhitha arrived with a glass of water from the kitchen.

She told her father, "This is the psychologist we saw on television."

"Oh yes! I just remembered. I'm glad to meet you, Dr.," her father said.

"Dr. Arnab," I corrected him.

"However, why are you here?" Her dad asked.

'I called him, Dad," Ankhitha said.

"Why, Molee?"

"To prove that I wasn't mistaken that day, that I actually witnessed the murder."

Her father looked at her and then at me with sorrowful eyes, then silently left with his wife and entered their bedroom. I could overhear some low-key conversations between her parents in their room.

"Dr. Arnab, I apologize for that," Ankhitha said.

"Ah, it's okay; they are parents, and they are concerned about you and your reputation," I responded.

"I know, but it's necessary. I have to prove that I actually saw that murder, and for that, I need your assistance."

"I will help." I said, "Have you noticed that your parents, especially your mother, seem to recognize me but not entirely?"

"Yes," Ankhitha said with a laugh, "My mom thought she met you at Shailaja's daughter's nuptials."

"Indeed, there is a hypothesis behind that."

"What hypothesis?"

"She thought I met her at a wedding because her memories became jumbled and a false memory was formed in her mind."

"My mom has that issue constantly."

"It happens to everyone, not just her."

"Has that ever happened to you before, like déjà vu?" Ankhitha looked thoughtful as she responded to my question.

"To be honest, sometimes, yeah," she replied.

"That phenomenon is called a false memory, also known as shuffled memories."

"It's an interesting theory."

"Possibly in the elevator or somewhere else, have you ever seen that victim before?"

"No, I didn't," I said emphatically.

"I want you to focus; don't rush to conclusions. Relax and close your eyes."

Ankhitha looked away.

"Inhale and exhale deeply, then think: Have you ever seen him before? Even a brief glimpse is enough."

After taking a deep breath and pausing for a moment, she opened her eyes.

"No, Doctor, I'm sure I never even caught a fleeting glimpse of him before the murder event."

I sighed and remained silent for a while; she gave me an odd glance.

I said, "Okay, let me see the room where you witnessed the crime."

"Absolutely, Mom!" Ankitha exclaimed enthusiastically.

"What?" Mom emerged from her bedroom, her expression showing anger.

Ankhitha explained, "I need the door key."

"It's right there," her mother replied, pointing to the rack in the main hallway cabinet. Ankhitha took the key from the shelf, and together we entered the room. As we stepped in, the gloominess of the room prompted me to turn on the light.

Sniffing, Ankhitha said, "I'm sorry, doctor, I have a dust sensitivity."

"It's fine. Where did you witness the murder? Can you show me the exact spot?" I inquired.

Ankhitha led me to the window and gestured toward block B's seventh level.

"Do these two buildings belong to the same category?" I asked.

"Yes, these two buildings are part of the same project."

"I'm curious about why they both look so similar," I mused, looking at the window on the seventh floor of the building across from us. Its darkness gave the impression of being deserted. I contemplated how to convince her that the event she had witnessed might have been a dream.

Suddenly, the doorbell of her flat rang. "Let me check who it is," Ankhitha said as she walked towards the front entrance.

Greeshma and Basi entered. Ankhitha welcomed them in and introduced me, saying, "Dr. Arnab, these are my buddies, Greeshma and Basi."

Ankhitha turned to Greeshma and Basi and introduced me, "And he is the psychologist, Dr. Arnab."

Basi asked, "Like Lalettan, the psychiatrist in 'Manichithrathazhu'?"

"Not exactly, I'm a psychologist," I clarified, choosing not to delve further into the difference.

Basi continued, "Aren't they the same?"

"Ankhitha called me here," I interjected, redirecting the conversation.

"Why?" Greeshma inquired, "Is it related to that murder incident?"

"Yes, it is," Ankhitha confirmed.

Basi scoffed, "So you've officially gone crazy."

In response, Ankhitha playfully punched Basi's arm. I chimed in, "Whatever the case, let's find out. Come on, let's enter the room where these events took place."

Greeshma and Basi entered the room, perching on the bed while giving me an odd look. Whispering in Ankhitha's ear, Greeshma asked, "Are you sure about him? What if he labels you as a mental patient?"

Hearing that, I chuckled. "I trust him," Ankhitha replied, displaying confidence in my abilities. After a while, Basi sat next to me, and we continued chatting.

"Why have we been waiting here for so long?" Basi finally asked.

I pondered how to make the situation more enjoyable and decided to entertain Basi by sharing myths.

In a hushed tone, I said to Basi, "Actually, we're waiting for a ghost."

"You're joking, right?" Basi replied, his tone puzzled and frightened after the sudden startle.

"I'm not joking, and not only that, I'm also a wizard," I added mischievously, "There's a ghost on the seventh floor of block B."

Basi's voice quivered as he responded, "No way, I'm not buying it."

As I drew closer, I murmured, "The ghost is right behind you."

Basi started to perspire, slowly turning around in terror.

"BOOOOOM!" Greeshma jumped at him, causing a great scare.

"What's wrong with you, you jerk? You scared the hell out of me!" Basi scolded Greeshma.

Laughter erupted as we poked fun at the situation.

"You guys are crazy," Basi chuckled, shaking his head.

After a while, I suggested, "Let's go to flat 7-B in block B; we might find something there."

Greeshma, Ankhitha, Basi, and I headed for the seventh floor of block B. I pressed the bell for 7C, and the door was opened by the same man with curly hair.

"Oh, it's this crazy lady again. What do you want now?" the man asked in annoyance.

I smiled and introduced myself, "I'm Dr. Arnab. We'd like to come in."

"Doctor? A psychiatrist?" he quipped.

"Psychologist, actually. Could you please let us in?" I requested.

"Why should I let you people in? To make fun of me again?"

I pleaded, "Please, it's a request."

"Fine, come in," he grumbled, allowing us inside.

"What's your name?" I asked him.

"Vikrant," he replied.

I noticed numerous cameras, lights, and other studio equipment around, as I had observed before.

"Are you a photographer?" I inquired.

"Professional cinematographer," Vikrant clarified.

"Wow," I exclaimed, looking around at the equipment. I then started examining smaller details, like the arrangement of the furniture in the main hall.

I turned to Ankhitha and asked, "What did you see in this room on that day? Be specific."

"I saw some briefcases, carton boxes, and a large mirror over there in the corner," Ankhitha recalled.

"I had them placed there temporarily because I was moving that day," Vikrant explained.

"What happened to that mirror now?" I questioned.

"I moved it into my room," Vikrant replied.

"Could you show me?" I asked, and Vikrant led me to his room. The large mirror covered an entire wall, reflecting the room in perfect detail.

"That's a clever design choice," I remarked.

"To give the illusion of a larger room," Vikrant explained.

"I remember seeing this mirror in the corner of the main hall," Ankhitha added.

"Yes, I initially had it on the balcony while I rearranged the furniture. Later that night, I was moving it from the balcony to the main hall. That's when you guys showed up out of nowhere, knocked on my door, and barged in as I opened it," Vikrant recounted.

"Just a moment," I said, struck by a thought. "You had the mirror on the balcony that day?"

"Yes," Vikrant confirmed.

I was amazed and rushed to the balcony. From there, I had a view of Ankitha's room. Vikrant followed me.

"What's going on, Dr.?" Greeshma asked, joining us.

I was astounded. "Ankhitha didn't dream that day; she actually witnessed the murder."

CHAPTER SEVEN

Greeshma, Ankhitha, Basi, and her parents gathered in the foyer of Ankhitha's apartment.

"What happened there? I got confused," Ankhitha said.

"I can see how that might be confusing. Let me explain," I said. "It has been proven that you witnessed the crime unfold just above your apartment in block A, not in block B."

"How did she manage to see a murder happening on the eighth floor of block A from the seventh floor of block B? That doesn't make any sense at all," Ankhitha's dad remarked.

"Actually, it does," I replied.

"How?" Ankhitha inquired.

"It's all about perspective. To understand, we need to determine the direction in which the lady swung the rod – was it to the right or to the left?"

"Let me think," Ankhitha contemplated for a moment. "I believe it was to the left."

"Good. Now, did that strike you as odd?" I asked.

"Yes, it did. She must have a left-handed swing, which is why she struck him from that angle," Ankhitha responded.

"Well, that's a valid observation, but what if I told you that she actually struck him in the right spot?" I challenged.

Ankhitha's father spoke up, "You're still perplexing us."

"Allow me to clarify," I said. "There's no confusion here. Vikrant had placed a mirror on the balcony that day."

Greeshma exclaimed in excitement, "So she saw the reflection from the eighth floor of block A, which was directly above Ankhitha's floor!"

"Exactly. You've got it," I affirmed, taking a marker pen and illustrating on the whiteboard. "Let me demonstrate once more."

Here, on the eighth level, the murder occurred.

The mirror was kept at Vikrant's apartment's balcony, which is set on the 7th level of block B.

7th floor, from where Ankhitha saw the murder

BLOCK B

BLOCK A

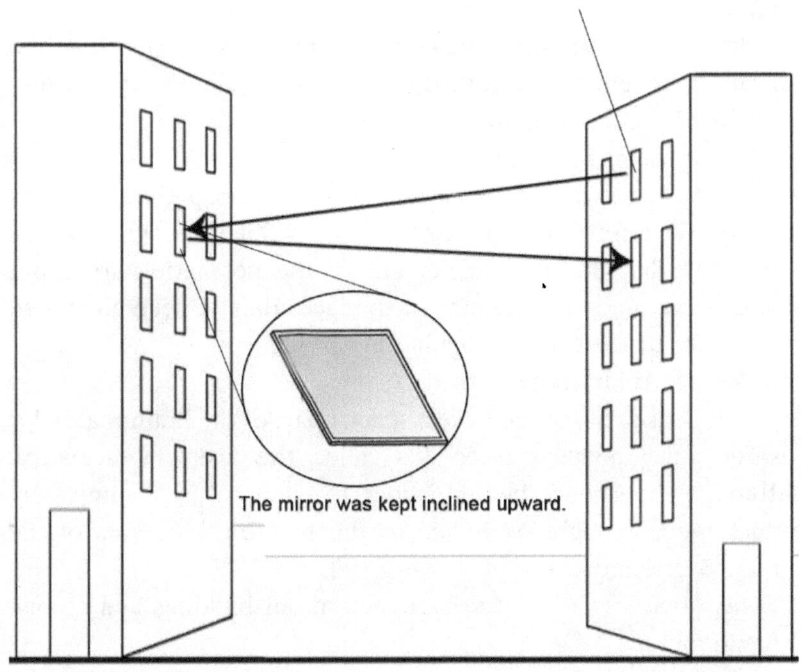

I gestured toward the seventh-floor window of Block B and said, "The mirror that Vikrant kept on the balcony was slightly tilted upward, causing the image of the murder that occurred on the eighth level to be transmitted to the seventh floor of Block B and reflected onto the seventh floor of Block A." I demonstrated.

"So, Ankhitha saw the reflection of the murder that took place on the 8th floor of our building, which is the 8th floor of Block A," Ankhitha's dad explained.

"Exactly," I confirmed.

"But how is it that she can still vividly recall the victim's face today? Even when I see someone every day, I tend to forget their face. She only had a fleeting glance at him, yet she remembers," Basi inquired.

"Remember, Ankhitha, the Punjabi man you saw in my clinic and instantly recognized, even though you had previously seen him in an article?" I asked Ankhitha.

"I do," Ankhitha replied.

"You possess a gift; that's why you can grasp their faces so swiftly. We refer to individuals like you as 'super recognizers.' It's estimated that one to two percent of the population are super recognizers, able to recall 80% of the faces they've seen compared to the 20% by the general population."

"Wow!" Ankhitha exclaimed.

"Yes, Ankhitha, we do have a special part of the brain that helps us recognize people's faces. It's called the fusiform face area. Although the science behind 'super recognition' isn't completely understood, it might be linked to the fusiform face area of the brain," I explained.

"My goodness, a murder happened in our building, and no one knew about it."

"Even though I was the only one to notice, I was still in the wrong place. By the time we realized it, the killer had destroyed all the evidence, and we were looking for them in Block B," Ankhitha spoke passionately.

I consoled her, "Ankhitha, it's not your fault."

"Yes, it is. When I had the chance to save him, none of you believed me. You were all busy trying to prove that I'm a crazy woman. And because of that, a life was lost," Ankhitha stormed off to her room.

Her parents broke down in tears.

"Don't worry, let me talk to her," I said, placing a sympathetic hand on her father's shoulder.

"My daughter endured so much that day, and I should have believed her," her father said, his voice filled with emotion.

Her mother sobbed, "I felt ashamed that day; I shouted at her."

"It's alright, anyone would have reacted similarly," I reassured, and I entered her room. She was sitting on the bed, crying, as I walked in. I sat down beside her, determined to uplift her spirits.

"Do you remember the story of the floating ship I told you?" I asked.

"Yeah, you didn't finish that," Ankhitha replied. "Why did the ship fly, and how did it manage to do that?"

"The ironic thing is that light also played a role in it. While in your case, you saw the reflection, in his case, it's known as a 'Fata Morgana.'"

"Fata Morgana?" Ankhitha questioned, furrowing her brow. "What is that?"

"A temperature inversion, also known as a Fata Morgana, occurs when cold, dense air near the Earth's surface gets trapped beneath a layer of warmer air above. This causes light rays from distant objects to bend downhill in the direction of an observer on the ground."

"That's profound and almost unbelievable. How can light bend?"

"There are many aspects of the world that we still don't fully understand."

"But still, it's hard to believe that light can bend."

"What if I were to say it was a ghost ship? Would you believe that?"

"Maybe, I suppose," Ankhitha said mockingly.

"That's exactly why charlatans exploit this. They make a lot of money deceiving people because many won't believe in facts," I said.

"That's true."

"You laughed when I brought up the Fata Morgana theory because you hadn't heard of it before, and your mind struggled to grasp it. The same thing happened when you told your parents about the murder. But once I provided the right explanation, they began to believe."

"They could have at least tried."

"When I told you about the Fata Morgana hypothesis, you could have given it a chance. Instead, you mocked me," I said.

Ankhitha looked down, distressed.

"It's a common human phenomenon. What we want to see and believe often precedes what we actually see."

We both fell silent for a moment. Then, Ankhitha stood up and gave me an intense look.

"I'm curious about that woman. She killed that poor man, and yet she's living a normal life. I'm the only one who knows it wasn't an accident but a murder. I wish I could look into her eyes and see the fear of a criminal. We have to bring her to court. Dr., you've been a great help to me. Will you stand by me?"

After hearing her words, I felt that this was the moment I had been waiting for. I could delve deeper into criminal behavior. Perhaps, in this instance, I could uncover more information related to my search. I extended my hand for a handshake. Ankhitha shook my hand after I assured her, "I'll be there with you."

CHAPTER EIGHT

There was a knocking sound. I pulled the blanket over myself and went to sleep because I didn't care. Gayathry, my sister, used to wake up early to study for her third-year medical examination. Gayathry entered my bedroom and woke me up.

"Gayathry, what's wrong with you?" I groaned and said, "Let me sleep."

Gayathry sneered, "I never thought my brother could be so lazy."

"Lazy? For what?" I asked as I turned to face her.

"Brother, there's an attractive girl here looking for you."

"A girl?" I stood up and peeked out the door's opening.

"Oh, that's Ankhitha," and I rushed to the cupboard to get a T-shirt.

"Ankhitha, interesting. The lady who used to send you private messages," Gayathry said.

"She's my patient, but not anymore."

"Come on, Chettayi, make her fall for you right now."

I told her to stop talking and started applying cologne.

"Chettayi, you forgot to brush your teeth. Otherwise, she might pull away from a kiss and leave."

I gave her a playful pinch on the arm and urged her, "Go to the kitchen and prepare a drink for her."

Gayathry replied, "I won't do that; I am not your servant."

I pleaded, "Please, I'll do anything for you."

She relented, "Fine," and walked out of the door. "Chettayi, are you in love?"

"Just leave," I commanded.

She said, "Okay, okay," and headed to the kitchen. I went to the bathroom and started brushing my teeth in the meantime. I returned and entered the main hall. I overheard my Amma and Ankhitha talking.

"Mole, are you married?" Amma asked.

"Aunty, I'm not," Ankhitha replied.

"Thank goodness," Amma muttered.

"Aunty?" Ankhitha asked a strange question.

"Nothing; I'm just looking for a girl for my..." Amma was about to finish when I abruptly interrupted.

I interrupted her, "Amma, Gayathry is calling you."

"Monee, give me a sec so I can talk to her," Amma said.

"Please, it's important, Amma," I pleaded.

"GAYATHRY, what's wrong with this girl?" Amma shouted and rushed to the kitchen. I went and sat down next to Ankhitha on the sofa.

"Your mom was talking about finding you a girl; what's the deal?" Ankhitha inquired.

"Nah, my mom is a typical Indian woman; She's always wanted me to get married as soon as possible," I explained.

"Well, I think you should get married because I think you're getting old."

"The truth is, I can't seem to find a girl who can put up with my quirks."

"What kind of woman are you looking for?"

"I really dislike this question."

"Why?"

"I'm not shopping for a product where I can demand specific features like we do when buying computers, such as 8 GB of RAM, a good graphics card, and so on. Let a woman be herself because she has her own feelings, interests, and personality."

"That's true, but don't we all have certain expectations of our partners?"

"What expectations? When circumstances change, our interests change too. For example, when I watch a movie, I remember how I once dreamed of becoming an actor. The right fit varies over time, and our priorities shift with it."

"Are you saying we shouldn't have any preconceived ideas about our partners, then?"

"I'm saying we should aim for compatibility with our partners; you felt compatible with me, and that's why you brought up your concern. I'm here to support you because of that."

Ankhitha gave me a thoughtful look as she considered my words. Mom emerged from the kitchen.

"Why are you deceiving me, Arnab? Gayathry didn't call me," stated Amma.

I remarked, "She's lying; you know Gayathry; she loves to play practical jokes on people." She scolded Gayathry in the kitchen again, and I started to chuckle.

"Why are you tricking your mother? That's not fair," Ankhitha said.

"Well, it's my way of showing them how much I care." I remarked, "We're more like best buddies."

"Still, this is too much."

"May I ask you one question? Have you ever played such tricks on your mother?"

"Never."

"Why?"

"Because she'd get irritated."

"All right, then, let me change my clothes; in the meantime, I need you to look something up on Google."

"Why is that?"

I said, "Let me change my clothes. By then, search for 'cute aggression'." I went to my room to change. The moment Ankhitha took out her phone, she opened the Google Chrome app and looked up 'cute aggression'. The search results appeared.

"Cute aggression" refers to the urge to squeeze, bite, or pinch something adorable, like a baby animal or a young human, without intending to harm them. Some individuals express their emotions in a bimodal way, meaning they display both positive and negative reactions in response to positive experiences.

I finished dressing and returned to the main hall.

"Why did you ask me to look into this?" Ankhitha asked.

"We'll discuss it later. First, let's investigate the woman who lost her husband," I said.

"Where can we find her, though?"

"It's directly above your apartment, so let's find out who lives on the eighth floor."

"It is; mine is 7B," she replied.

"Let's go see her at 8-B

I started the car's engine and accelerated. Seated next to me was Ankhitha.

"What can we discover if we go to her apartment?" Ankhitha asked. Prior to that, I suggested, "Well, we should find out who resides there; we need to gather information about her."

"Where can we find that?"

"From the news report you told me about the incident, and let's also inquire further about her from the apartment's caretaker."

"I have the newspaper with me," Ankhitha said, taking it out of her handbag.

"Read it."

"*Anwar Zubair, the head of Al Zubair Building Materials, passed away on July 20th after the Hyundai i20 he was driving collided with a tree in the Anaikatti area of Palakkad district. The collision occurred near the Attapadi Reserve Forest during the early hours of the morning. A fierce thunderstorm and heavy rainfall had swept through the region, uprooting trees and leaving the area without electricity for the night. He had checked in at the "Komaram Lodge" motel in Anakkatti at 6:00 a.m. on July 19th and left the following morning.* "

"Stop, stop," I interrupted. "Read the last line again."

"He arrived at the "Komaram Lodge" motel in Anakkatti on July 19th at 6:00 AM and left the following morning," Ankhitha read.

"You said you witnessed the murder at 2 AM, correct?" I asked.

"Yes, I do recall, because July 19th was my birthday. It was July 19th, after 2 AM."

"If so, how did he get there and stay at a motel in Pallakad District from Thrissur?"

"That's what puzzled me as well."

"This situation is trickier than I anticipated."

"That's right, everything is turned around," Ankhitha yelled angrily.

"Don't worry, we'll figure it out," I reassured her as I continued to drive. We reached Ankhitha's apartment together. The security officer stopped us, noted my vehicle's license plate in a ledger, and then unlocked the gate for us. I parked my vehicle in a designated spot.

"Let's start by questioning the security guard about the resident of 8-B," I said.

"How would he know?"

"Don't underestimate them; they always keep an eye on all the residents here."

I addressed the security officer, "Hey, I'm with Ankhitha."

"Ha! Ankhitha mole, how are you?" the security guard greeted her.

Ankhitha responded, "Uncle, I'm fine."

"So, your employment situation is satisfactory?" I asked the security officer.

"Yeah, earning a good salary and taking care of these people are my main priorities in this position. I have to do it."

"True. Can I ask you a question then?" I inquired.

The security guard replied, "Sure, sir."

"Can you tell me more about the resident of 8-B?" I asked. The security guard gave Ankhitha a skeptical glance.

"You are free to tell him," Ankhitha said.

"Sir, the property was purchased by a Muslim. His real name is Raees Mohammed," the security guard said.

"Is he staying here?"

"No, but his daughter does; her name is Linsha Zubair."

"Zubair? Her spouse?"

"Maybe. I've never seen her spouse here. She has been residing here for three years. Her father had previously rented out his flat."

"Okay, but where is the caretaker?"

"He might be in the office right now."

I handed him 100 rupees that I had taken out of my purse and urged him to take it.

The guard said, "God bless you, son." We both went to the office. Outside the office, the caretaker was lounging on a couch.

"Hey, Ankhitha," the caretaker turned to face me and asked, "who is this gentleman?"

Ankhitha said, "He is my friend. He would like to talk to you."

"What should we talk about?"

"Actually, Linsha Zubair is the person I would like to talk about, who stays in 8-B; she is Mohammed Raees's child."

"Yes, I am aware of her; she has been living here for three years. What information do you want to know about her?"

"Anything you know about her relatives."

"What is it that you want to know?" he asked. I waited silently for some time as I crafted a story in my mind.

"Well, I'd like to purchase that flat, so I'm just asking," I said.

"Oh! Mohammed Raees is someone I know. I only know he's an NRI; that's all. He operates a company there."

"Is it true that Linsha is married?"

"I heard her spouse passed away in a car accident years ago; it was a very tragic time for her, poor lady."

"His name?" I inquired.

He said, "Zubair, I believe," as he was thinking. "Oh yes, Anwar Zubair."

"Okay. Raees had just one child, right?"

"No, I've never seen his son, who is one of his other children. I only know he is a medical student. Raees mentioned him once during our conversation."

"All right, thanks," I said. "Let me go meet her."

I went to the elevator with Ankhitha. Suddenly, Basi entered from the main entrance. "Oh, goodness! You two again?" he said sarcastically.

"You are such an ass; you rushed away yesterday," Ankhitha remarked.

"A ghost?" Ankhitha inquired.

"My sorcerous ability has detected that the spirit is pursuing you," I mockingly said. "Be cautious."

"I wish the apparition was a girl. How long can I remain single?" Basi said as the elevator doors slid open after he finished speaking. Ankhitha pressed the seventh floor button, while Basi pressed the fifth.

"You idiot, it's 7, Ankhitha, not 8," Basi said.

"Just keep to yourself, idiot," Ankhitha commanded.

Basi left as the fifth floor arrived. Before the elevator's sliding door could shut, he extended his middle finger to Ankhitha.

Ankhitha sneered, "Such an imbecile." I laughed hysterically. She glared fiercely at me and questioned, "What?"

I uttered, "Nothing," while covering my mouth with my hand. When the elevator reached the eighth floor, we both got out and knocked on the door of 8-B.

"What are we going to do then? What do we want to ask?" Ankhitha muttered something.

"I would approach her pretending to be Anwar Zubair's friend," I said.

A short while later, a woman wearing gym attire and with long, straight hair opened the door. Contrary to what we might have expected based on her name, she appeared very modern.

"Yes, who are you guys?" the lady asked, and it was evident that she had been working out, given her heavy breathing.

I said, "Um, I'm Anwar Zubair's school friend, so I came to see you."

She gave me an odd look, and her slightly terrified eyes granted us entry. The interior of the apartment seemed to be beautifully designed.

"Did you design the furniture here?" I asked.

"I did," the lady replied.

I remarked, "Mrs Linsha Zubair, it's really lovely."

"It's Miss Linsha now," she said.

"Ah, yes! I heard about your husband's passing last week. He was in my class. I couldn't help but come to see you," I said.

Ankhitha glared angrily at the woman as she rubbed her palms with her thumbs.

"I'll have a glass of water, please," I requested.

"Sure," Linsha said as she entered the kitchen.

I approached Ankhitha and said in a low voice, "Stop looking at her like that."

Ankhitha said in a low voice, "Look at her; she's so happy even after killing her husband."

"We're not sure about that, and don't make her wary of our presence," I cautioned.

"I'm positive it's her," Ankhitha insisted. "The woman who killed him also had long hair like her."

"Just stop staring at her, whatever it is. She's coming, so be quiet."

Linsha brought two cups of water, first giving one to Ankhitha and then to me. After taking it, I sat on the couch and motioned for Miss Linsha to join me. Her hands were trembling slightly, and she sat down on the couch with a fearful look.

I inquired, "Miss Linsha, how did Anwar die?"

"What?" she exclaimed, suddenly turning to face me in fear.

I repeated, "How did that accident happen?"

"Oh! My husband had a habit of driving fast, especially at night when it was dark and there were no streetlights," Linsha said, looking down. "I didn't realize that was his last day."

"Where were you when the accident happened on July 20th?" I queried.

"I... I was in a grocery shop," Linsha replied, looking at me with a startled expression.

Usually, people shed a tear or two when talking about their deceased loved ones, but she seemed more frightened than sorrowful. I noticed a family picture frame on the TV table, picked it up, and asked, "Is this your family?"

She got to her feet when she saw me picking it and said, "Yes. This is my Vappachi, Ummachi, and my little brother," pointing at each of them in the picture.

I asked, "Where are they now?"

"Ummachi and Vappachi went to Dubai. My brother is currently a student at Anpal Medical College," Linsha stated.

"What is the name of the aspiring doctor?" I questioned.

"Oh! Baaqir Raees."

I carefully examined his photo, placed the frame back on the table, and asked, "Which batch is he in?"

"2016," she said.

"He had several supplementary exams, didn't he? My sister also studies at Jubilee Medical College; she belongs to the 2018 batch."

She exclaimed, "Oh, good."

Glancing at my watch, I said, "Oh, it's late. Let me go. It was nice to meet you, Linsha," extending my hand for a handshake. Her palm met mine, and we shook hands.

Ankhitha and I left Linsha's apartment together and entered the elevator.

"We didn't ask her anything about the murder," Ankhitha said, pressing the seventh-floor button.

"Shh, quiet," I said. "We didn't ask any questions, but Linsha herself revealed most of the information."

We got out of the elevator and rang the doorbell to Ankhitha's apartment.

"Revealed what?" Ankhitha inquired.

"I'll tell you, dear," I said as Ankhitha's mother opened the door.

"Oh, come settle down, you two. You should try my chicken biriyani today, Doctor," her mother said.

I joked, "I hope there won't be any poison in it."

"Doctor, I apologize for that," Ankhitha's mom expressed regret to me.

I sat down on the couch after saying, "It's alright, aunty; I took it as a joke."

Ankhitha's dad emerged from his bedroom. He shook my hand and took a seat next to me.

Ankhitha irritatedly asked me, "Please tell me what she revealed."

"Hey, be calm. It's clear that Linsha was involved in the murder," I said.

"How did you confirm that?" Ankhitha asked.

"Indeed, whenever we talk about or ponder a loved one who has passed away, we often experience sadness and begin to weep."

"Of course," Ankhitha said.

"I realised she wasn't depressed; she was terrified. Her hands were shaking, and she began to faintly perspire."

"I didn't notice that," Ankhitha said.

I said, "I'm a psychologist, and it's my responsibility to observe my patients' body language to figure out what issue they're facing."

"Did the supposed murder actually happen there?" Ankhitha's dad inquired.

I stated, "The facts support it."

Ankhitha said, "She's such an intruder that somehow she covered up everything."

"Well, I disagree. I assert that she wasn't the one who hushed it up."

"Why is that so?" Ankhitha asked.

"She is a novice and has an emotive character. While we were meeting her, she was unable to hide her feelings. She had the option of emulating a depressed wife who had lost her spouse, but she didn't. There is someone there who helped her cover the crime she committed."

"Who could it be?"

"Her family members, such as her father, mother, or sibling, or possibly a lover."

"I‘m sure it’s her lover. What other motive could a woman have for killing her husband?" said Ankhitha.

I chuckled and remarked, "There might be a lot more motives; I can’t draw any conclusions from this. Only a chance exists."

"So what might be the motive?"

"We must ascertain that. We need to know ’WHEN,‘ ’WHERE,‘ ’WHY,‘ and ’HOW‘ in order to prove the murder. We are aware of ’when,‘ ’where,‘ and ’how.‘ The funny thing is, we have no evidence for it at the moment; all we have is speculation. The rest will fall into our laps automatically if we can figure out WHY first."

"How do we prove our speculation?"

"We must first learn about their marriage situation. According to the caretaker, her spouse has never stayed with her here. She was always by herself. We need to ask her friends, family members, and anyone else who is close to them. Therefore, we must travel to her homeland."

"How do we locate her home country?"

"I will find out."

"I find it hard to believe a woman could murder her husband," Ankhitha’s dad said.

"Despite the fact that she resides in our building, how come we were unaware of her presence?" Ankhitha asked.

"There are more than 200 people who reside in this building, so it’s impossible to get to know everyone," Ankhitha’s dad explained.

I checked Linsha’s Instagram profile at the same time. As soon as I had her profile, I looked at Baaqir, her younger brother, as well as her parents’ Instagram accounts. Because the person in the photo on Baaqir’s Instagram page was the same as the one I saw in Linsha’s home, the photo where it was kept next to the TV, I was able to identify him. On my phone, I took a screenshot of each person’s Instagram profile.

Ankhitha’s mom brought a platter of chicken biriyani out of the kitchen and handed it to me. I tasted it.

"Mmm... it’s delicious."

CHAPTER NINE

We all cherish our leisure and serenity on Sundays. Given my lifelong dedication to researching criminal psychology, Ankhitha's situation was more than just my duty—it was my passion. To learn more about Linsha Zubair, we decided to visit her homeland. Ankhitha's dad, being a respected person, had no trouble obtaining Mohammed Raees's homeland address through a friend who works at Skyline Flat Company. Therefore, Ankhitha and I decided to travel together, and we invited Greeshma and Basi to join us. I received a call from Ankhitha at 8:00 on Sunday morning.

"Where are you?" Ankhitha inquired over the phone.

I hadn't gotten out of bed yet but replied, "I'm on my way."

"We're ready. Come quickly," Ankhitha urged.

"I'll be there in ten minutes," I assured her and hung up the phone.

I hastily put on some clothes and headed to the dining area to grab some food. Gayathry was also preparing to leave.

"Where are you going, Gayathry?" I asked.

Gayathry responded, "I planned to go on a trip with my friends and asked my Achan for permission."

"Acha!" I exclaimed, addressing my father.

"What happened? Why are you screaming?" my father inquired.

"Did you give her permission to go with her friends?" I asked, winking at him playfully to tease Gayathry.

My father answered, "Ahhh... ummm... no." Gayathry shot him a displeased look.

I said in a teasing tone, "Well, you shouldn't go, then," just to annoy her.

Gayathry began pleading with my father, saying, "Acha, please, I want to go, please."

"He's just teasing you. You're free to go, molee," my father said. Gayathry displayed a cute, irritated expression. Amma eventually arrived and set the food on the dining room table.

"Chettayi, where are you going?" Gayathry asked in a suspicious tone.

I remarked, "I'm going on a trip with my friends."

"Friends or a girlfriend?" Gayathry inquired.

"Girlfriend?" Achan questioned, looking skeptical.

"Chettayi does have a girlfriend, Acha. Her name is Ankhitha," Gayathry sarcastically remarked.

I retorted, "No, acha, she's just playing."

"I wouldn't mind if you had a girlfriend, as long as she's nice," Achan said.

I remarked, "She's just one of my patients."

Gayathry mockingly referred to her as "the patient who secretly messages him."

"You've been teasing me about this for a long time; what's wrong with you? YES! She is my girlfriend. Do you have a problem with it?" I said.

Gayathry responded, "No, actually, we're thrilled about it."

"You're crazy," I said as I got up and headed for the washbasin.

Amma said, "Mone, eat some food."

Gayathry mockingly said, "Amma, no need because Chettayi wants to dine with Ankhitha." To refute her claims, I returned, ate my food quickly, and said, "Should I drop you somewhere?" as I turned to Gayathry.

"There's no need, chettayi; I won't intrude on your date. I'll go by myself," Gayathry chuckled in response.

I got up, washed my hands at the washbasin, grabbed the car keys, and left the house.

"Definitely has a girlfriend," Amma said.

Outside their flat, Ankhitha, Basi, and Greeshma were waiting. I had brought a seven-seater Innova for our journey, and they all entered as I pulled up close to them.

"Is Dr. joining us, too?" Basi asked with a hint of fear.

"Yes, he is. Any problem, bro?" I questioned.

Basi responded, "Nope, nothing." I could sense that he didn't expect me to come and was a bit disappointed, so I was slightly suspicious of him.

"So, where is Linsha's place?" I inquired, looking at Ankhitha.

Ankhitha replied, "Cochin, close to Panambally Nagar."

I said, "Set up the GPS."

"LET'S GOOOOO!" Basi screamed, and a Malayalam song, "Lejavathiye," started playing. I started driving the vehicle.

"In order to learn more about her, what are we going to do?" Ankhitha asked.

"The first thing we need to know is how their marriage was. Typically, neighbors or family members will have information about that. Most people will try to find their weaknesses. We can dig into that," I explained.

"This trip is going to be boring because you guys are just going to meet her. Please drop me off at Lulu Mall," Basi requested.

"What will you do at Lulu Mall?" Greeshma asked.

"I'll hang around. Come if you want to," Basi said.

Greeshma replied, "No need; I'll stay with Ankhitha."

"Okay," Basi said and turned up the volume.

Greeshma playfully pinched his arm and said, "Basi, stop pestering us."

Basi responded, "Ahh, stop pinching my arm. What did I do?"

"Please be quiet," Greeshma advised.

"Oh, it's not just an 'investigation' trip, I see. Let him have fun however he wants to. Basi, go ahead and do whatever you want," I said.

"That's my brother in..." Basi started to say but then abruptly stopped. Slowly, we began to enjoy the trip, and later, we found humor in Basi's irritation. During the three-hour journey, I had flashbacks to my college days. Oh, how I wish time travel were possible!

We arrived at the LuLu Mall to drop Basi off, and he exited the car.

"Hey, take it. I made it for you," Greeshma offered him a sandwich.

Basi looked puzzled and asked, "What the heck is this?"

Greeshma replied, "Your favorite sandwich."

"Ah! I'm heading to McDonald's to get a Maharaja Burger, so there's no need," Basi replied, closing the car door behind him as he hurried into the LuLu Mall's entrance. Greeshma left the sandwich on the seat and fell silent for a moment. As I drove, I glanced at her through the rearview mirror. She appeared a bit teary and distraught.

Ankhitha, looking at the navigator, said, "We have 12 more minutes to Linsha's house."

I said, "Alright, let's go."

We eventually arrived at Linsha's home, a small and elegant house with two floors.

"It's a lovely home," Ankhita commented.

"Yes, and the gate is locked from the outside," I noted.

"No one lives around here?" Ankhitha asked.

"In Dubai, they reside. Only Linsha and her sibling are still in Kerala because her brother is studying MBBS here," I explained.

A man wearing a white cotton dhoti and a white half-sleeve shirt passed by us, appearing quite authoritative. As far as we know, Mohammed Raees is a well-known person, and activists often get to know NRIs well, as they are prominent in their home countries.

I addressed him as "Chetta" and asked, "Does no one live here?"

"Our Raees Mohammed resides here. He is a Dubai resident. Who are you exactly?" he inquired.

I quickly concocted a lie and said, "I am his daughter's friend, and I came here to deliver something. I thought Linsha might be here."

"Oh, Linsha? Are you talking about the girl who lost a substantial amount of money on a business that quickly failed?" he asked.

I inquired, "What business?"

"Some sort of interior design business, and as usual, girls should focus on serving their husbands rather than trying to be like men," he remarked.

"Oh! Chetta, is she here?" I asked.

"No, she rarely stays in this place. I haven't seen her since her husband passed away," he replied.

"Is there anyone close to her?" I probed.

"There's a girl over there; I've seen them together every time," he said, pointing to a nearby home. "They seemed to be close friends. Her name is Priya, and she was a partner in that failed business."

"Alright, thank you, Chetta," I said before starting the car and parking it near Priya's house. We all got out of the car.

"How can he say that women should serve their husbands and not try to be like men? We have the freedom to live however we like," Ankhitha muttered angrily.

"It seems that some locals still use outdated cultural stereotypes. Ah, just ignore it," Greeshma advised.

I suggested, "Let's go to that market."

"Why? Aren't we here to meet this girl?" Ankhitha inquired.

I said, "First, let's visit this market and buy something," and we proceeded there.

Ankhitha overheard Greeshma whisper to her, "I sometimes find his behavior strange."

Greeshma replied, "Shhh."

I yelled to both of them, "GIRLS, COME IN."

"Weird," Greeshma remarked, and they both entered. I took them to a gift shop.

"Select anything," I told them.

"Why?" Ankhitha asked.

"Just do it," I insisted.

Ankhitha pointed to a lovely brown plush bear, and I asked the salesperson to put it in a gift box.

"Are you buying a gift for someone?" Ankhitha inquired.

"Yes," I replied.

"For whom?" she asked.

I playfully told her, "For my lover," just for amusement.

"Oh!" Ankhitha responded, crossing her arms and avoiding my gaze, indicating that she might have felt a bit uncomfortable when I said that. The gift was wrapped, so I took it.

"Let's go to Linsha's friend's place," I said, and they followed.

When we entered the gate of Priya's home, we saw a beautiful garden. They seemed to be quite knowledgeable about plants. We knocked on the door and were greeted by a young child, perhaps 7 or 8 years old.

"Mummyyyyyyy!" the child shouted and ran inside to call her mother. A woman in a maxi dress holding a slotted turner came out of the kitchen.

"Yes, who are you guys?" she asked.

"I was a close friend of Linsha's husband," I said.

"Oh!"

"I came here to meet Linsha and give her this gift. Zubair used to give my address for online purchases before. Linsha unintentionally placed this order by clicking on my address. Since there was no one at Linsha's home, I decided to give it to you," I lied to persuade her.

Greeshma muttered to Ankhitha, "He said he bought this gift for his lover."

Ankhitha shushed her, "Sshhhh."

"Oh, okay, I'll keep it and give it to her when she comes. You guys traveled quite a distance to come here," the woman said.

"Yes, we made a three-hour drive just to deliver this. I didn't have Linsha's phone number."

"Oh my goodness, please come and sit. I'll serve each of you three lime juices," she said and went back to the kitchen.

I said, "Thank you," and the three of us sat down on the sofa.

"You look very familiar to me; where have we met?" the woman asked.

I fabricated a response, saying, "Perhaps at Zubair's wedding."

"Your name?" she inquired.

"I am Arnab, Dr. Arnab."

"Doctor? Like a surgeon?"

"I am a psychologist."

"Oh! I'm Priya. And you two?" She turned to Greeshma and Ankhitha.

They both introduced themselves, "I am Greeshma," "I am Ankhitha."

I said, "They are my friends."

Priya said, "Oh."

As I sipped my drink, I asked, "How long have you two been friends?"

"She finished the 10th grade at a school in Dubai. She came here for the 11th and 12th grades and joined my school. That's how we got really close."

"So, even before her marriage, you two were close."

"We naturally share everything with each other. I used to envy her a lot. She had a wonderful marriage."

"A wonderful marriage?" I asked, surprised.

"Yes! Why the shock?" Priya inquired.

"It's rare to find such a loving couple in this generation," I said.

"That's true. But their bond was truly amazing," Priya remarked.

"Would you mind sharing their story with us?" I asked.

"Of course! I was lonely and bored here, but at least I have someone to talk to now."

"Yes, we're in no hurry to leave either. I love hearing love stories."

"So, let me begin," Priya said excitedly and started telling Linsha and Zubair's story.

CHAPTER TEN

Priya speaks

Me and Linsha enrolled in an interior design degree program in Thrissur after completing our higher secondary education. Unfortunately, her father had already rented out their flat in Thrissur, so we couldn't stay there. Instead, we chose to reside in a girls' hostel near Kurianchira to be closer to her Skyline flat. During our college days, we explored almost every corner of Thrissur, making those days incredibly exciting.

On November 13, 2017, one of our classmates, Nimisha, had her wedding, and we all traveled to Alappuzha to attend it. Nimisha insisted that Linsha and I dance, so we did. The dance was a Dandiya, where men and women in vibrant attire danced together to the rhythms of the dholak and tabla. It was a joyful and energetic performance. It was during this dance that Anwar Zubair had his first interaction with Linsha. Anwar seemed captivated by Linsha as they danced together, but she remained unaware of his fixation on her. After the dance, we headed to the food area to eat, and that's when I noticed Anwar sitting at a nearby table.

I told Linsha, "The man in the maroon sherwani has been gazing at you for a while."

"Who?" Linsha inquired, turning her gaze towards him.

"Hey, don't look at him like that," I advised.

Linsha asked, "Then how should I look at him?"

"Don't let him know you're looking at him; just give him a subtle glance," I suggested. She turned and gave him a discreet look.

Linsha cynically remarked, "He's quite good-looking."

"Yes, and he's been looking at you," I said.

"Just ignore him; he'll go away," Linsha suggested.

We both stood up to walk to the outdoor wash station, and to my surprise, Anwar followed us. While Linsha and I were washing our hands, her phone suddenly fell to the ground.

"Be careful," Anwar said as he picked up her phone and handed it to her.

"Thanks," Linsha replied and hurried towards the auditorium hall, holding my hand.

"He's starting to follow us now," I observed.

"I'll definitely give him a piece of my mind if he does it again," Linsha remarked.

After some time, Linsha and I went up on stage to take pictures with the bride and groom.

"Nimisha, who's that man in the maroon sherwani over there?" Linsha asked her.

"Oh, that's Anwar. He's my cousin. Why do you ask?" Nimisha inquired.

"Is he a womanizer? He's been following us for a while," Linsha commented.

"No, he's never done that. He might just like you. Should I talk to him?" Nimisha offered.

"Just tell him to stop following me," Linsha replied before leaving the stage.

We then made our way to the ice cream section of the auditorium, and to our surprise, Anwar reappeared before us. I tried to stop Linsha, but she was visibly irritated and approached him.

"You know, I don't want to make a scene because you're Nimisha's cousin, and I don't want to tarnish your image. But please stop following me and staring at me. It's a request, so please comply," Linsha told him before turning away.

Anwar called her, "Excuse me, madam." Linsha turned back to face him.

Linsha asked, "Yes?"

He walked up to Linsha and asked, "Have you ever seen a rainbow between two majestic mountains?"

Linsha replied, somewhat puzzled, "No."

"What would you do if you had the chance to see that? What would be your reaction?" Anwar inquired.

"I would probably just look at it," Linsha replied.

"Why would you look at it?" Anwar asked.

"To appreciate its beauty," Linsha replied.

"Well, that's exactly what I'm doing; I'm appreciating your beauty by looking at you," Anwar said with a wink and then walked away.

I was taken aback by what he said, and for a moment, Linsha stood completely still. Then she turned to me and laughed.

"He's an absolute goofball," Linsha remarked.

I responded, "Nah, that was just a playful flirtatious line."

Linsha said, "BLAHH."

Two days later, Linsha and I were at the hostel, watching a movie called 'Lucifer.' Linsha's phone rang, and the caller was Nimisha. She took the call, and I became curious about their conversation, so I approached her.

"Why did she ask for your father's phone number?" I inquired.

"I have no idea. Come on, let's watch the movie," Linsha replied as she sat on the bed.

The next day, after our lectures were over, I was about to start my scooter when Linsha's father called her. She stepped aside to take the call, and I noticed she appeared tense while speaking with him. She returned and sat behind me as we headed to a coffee shop. Linsha remained silent in the coffee shop for a while.

"Hey, what happened? Why so quiet?" I asked.

"Do you remember the guy we met at Nimisha's wedding?" Linsha inquired.

"Nimisha's cousin, Anwar," I replied.

"Yeah, his parents called my dad."

"What? Why?"

"For a marriage proposal."

"How did they get your dad's phone number?"

"Nimisha gave it to them."

"So, that's why she called you last night and asked for your dad's phone number."

"Yes."

"Go and marry him, he's cute."

"Are you insane? Don't you remember that we both want to start our dream business together?"

"Yeah, to run an interior design firm with other professionals."

"Yes, and that won't happen if I get married soon."

"Then discuss it with your parents."

"They won't listen, and they've already inquired about his family. His renowned and wealthy family has already won my parents over."

"Dude, even after your marriage, we can still continue with our company."

"It's not that simple, Priya. What if he orders me not to pursue it to show his authority?"

"What authority?"

"The husband's authority."

"Are you kidding me? It's the 21st century. Spouses are considered equals."

"From a legal perspective, yes, but in many traditional societies, the husband is still seen as more important than his wife, and some people still hold onto those beliefs."

"Anyway, if you don't want to marry him, just say no."

"Just to meet him, my parents are flying back from Dubai."

"So, this time, your parents are taking it seriously."

"Yeah, and he's planned to meet me tomorrow at Shobha City Mall with his family. My father asked me to meet them the day after tomorrow."

"Holy crap."

"What should I do?"

"Meet him and politely decline."

"I'll give Baaqir a call."

"Your brother?"

As Linsha picked up her phone to call Baaqir, she replied, "Yes."

"Hello, where the hell are you?" Linsha asked on the phone.

Baaqir answered, "Heyyyy sister, I heard you got a boyfriend."

"He's not my boyfriend; listen carefully. I have no desire to marry him."

"Lol. My sweet sister, it's too late. My father asked me to be with you tomorrow at Shobha City Mall."

"I don't want to!" Linsha exclaimed.

"Lady, take it easy; let's meet him tomorrow. Tell him you don't want to marry him."

"Whatever the situation may be, I will not accept this proposal."

Baaqir said on the phone, "Your wish," and then he hung up.

I said, "Dude, just say no."

Linsha replied, "I'll do that."

I said, "Okay."

"Okay," Linsha responded.

I mockingly asked, "Okey?"

Linsha shouted, "Just shut the f*** up!"

The next day, I asked, "Where are you?" Linsha inquired.

"I'm on my way," Baaqir responded.

Linsha growled, "I know you're still in bed."

"From my hostel, it will only take 15 minutes to get to Shobha City Mall," Baaqir said.

"Come quickly," Linsha urged before hanging up the phone. In the Shobha City Mall's food court, Linsha and I waited together. We had both arrived early, waiting for Anwar and his family who were scheduled to arrive at 4 o'clock. Linsha was wearing a contemporary black dress with panels.

I complimented her, saying, "You look really beautiful today."

"Thank you," Linsha replied with a smile.

"But you're dressed quite modern, which might make you look a bit out of place for a Desi gathering. Typically, women wear a salwar kameez for such occasions," I remarked.

"I intentionally wore it to discourage this marriage proposal," Linsha explained.

"Wow, that's clever, dude."

Linsha said, "I know," and then her phone rang. It was her brother on the line.

Baaqir said, "I'm here at the game center."

Linsha said, "What on earth are you doing there? Idiot, come here to the food court."

"Wait," Baaqir mumbled, holding the call. He said, "Hello," after a brief pause.

"Yes, tell me," Linsha replied.

"Where are you guys? I'm over at the food court," Baaqir said.

Seeing him, I pointed my finger and said, "There he is."

Linsha said, "Turn around." Baaqir turned and waved at us. He joined us after hanging up the phone.

"You look very hot today, sista," Baaqir said.

Linsha chuckled, "Thank you, thank you."

"It's a formal meeting with the girl, not a date," Baaqir joked.

I informed him, "She's trying to sabotage this marriage proposal."

"I don't think our father will cancel this proposal. Anwar's family background and ancestors have greatly impressed our parents," Baaqir stated.

"Ancestors? Are they from a royal family or something?" Linsha laughed.

"I don't know. According to dad, they come from a royal lineage," Baaqir said.

"The era of royalty is long gone. We live in a democratic country now," Linsha commented.

"But for our parents, it seems like the era of kingdoms is still alive," Baaqir remarked.

Linsha sighed and said, "Whatever," in frustration.

"It's already four o'clock. Where are they?" I asked.

Baaqir said, "My dad gave them my number." Baaqir's phone suddenly rang, and the ringtone was a peculiar Tamil song.

Linsha questioned, "What kind of ringtone is that?"

Baaqir answered the call, saying, "Hello... Yes, uncle... The food court is where we are... Uncle, okay, uncle, we will wait."

"What are they saying?" Linsha inquired.

"They're on their way and will be here soon," Baaqir replied.

"Let's mess things up," Linsha said.

Baaqir's phone rang again after a while.

Answering the call, Baaqir said, "Hello, where are you, uncle?" ... "Yes, I saw you," he replied as he turned toward the escalator. He waved to an older man with a bald head and a business shirt. There was an older woman, presumably his mother, wearing a shiny saree, and Anwar, who was dressed in a stylish jacket that appeared to be leather.

I whispered to Linsha, "He actually looks really handsome."

Linsha shrugged and whispered back, "Yeah, whatever."

Baaqir gave them a handshake as they approached, introducing himself, "Hello, I'm Baaqir."

"I'm Zubair, and this is my wife, Ameena Zubair," he said, indicating his wife. Pointing to Anwar, he added, "This is my son Anwar."

Anwar's mother approached Linsha and introduced herself.

"Linsha, right?" Ameena Zubair inquired.

"Yes, aunty," Linsha replied. Then, to Linsha's surprise, Ameena Zubair gave her a stern look.

"I also enjoy it when my son likes modern women. So beautiful," Ameena exclaimed as she began to touch Linsha's cheek.

Linsha looked at her in shock, as she had expected quite the opposite reaction. In many Indian families, women are expected to dress traditionally, but in this case, they seemed to be very open-minded individuals. We all then proceeded to a restaurant in the mall.

As Anwar's mother turned toward me, she asked, "Is this your friend, Linsha?"

Linsha introduced me, saying, "Yes, aunty, this is my friend Priya."

I greeted her with a smile, saying, "Hello."

Ameena Zubair remarked, "Hello, dear."

"You two must be Nimisha's classmates," Anwar's father inquired.

Linsha confirmed, "Yes, uncle."

Anwar added, "We met at Nimisha's wedding."

"Yes, she danced on stage, I remember that. Since then, I've been praying to God for you to become my daughter-in-law," Anwar's father declared.

It seemed that, at least in their minds, this union between their son and Linsha had been preordained. Linsha had made many attempts to derail this marriage proposal, but everything was turning out quite the opposite of what she had expected. I couldn't help but chuckle at every turn.

"So, Baaqir, you're pursuing an MBBS degree now?" Anwar's father asked.

Baaqir replied, "Yes, uncle."

"Could you please treat me? I think I have a respiratory issue," Anwar's father requested with a grin.

Baaqir nervously responded, "Uncle, I'm in my first year."

"You became a doctor for us the moment you entered medical college," Anwar's father remarked, making us all laugh. Following that, Baaqir was compelled to eat as Anwar's parents coaxed him into it.

"Do you want to speak with Anwar privately?" Anwar's father inquired after a while.

Linsha replied, "Yes, definitely. Come with us, Priya."

"Why should I come with you while you guys are leaving?" I asked.

"Please do as I say. Come with me," Linsha whispered.

So, to talk privately, Linsha, Anwar, and I moved to a different table. Meanwhile, Anwar's parents were engrossed in conversation with Baaqir.

"My parents are very good with kids; that's why they're treating Baaqir that way," Anwar explained.

Linsha replied, "I can see that."

"You'll get used to it after marriage," Anwar remarked.

"Yeah," Linsha sighed. "Speaking of that, I need to tell you something."

"We have our whole lives to share things, Linsha," Anwar said.

"I'm sorry, but I really liked your parents, and you're a great guy. However, I really don't want to get married right now," Linsha explained.

Anwar asked, "Why not?"

"We have a vision, me and Priya. We want to start our own business. This marriage could derail our dream. Please understand."

"You know, I hate losing," Anwar said in a slightly threatening tone.

"I'm sorry?" Linsha nervously replied.

"Ah, what I meant to say is that I can help you with your business. Money is not an issue for us. You can rely on our financial support."

"Well, I appreciate your generosity. However, we want to build the business on our own. Please forget about me. You'll find a wonderful girl who you truly want." Linsha took my hand, stood up, and walked over to his family. I heard a cup shatter behind me. When I turned around, I saw a broken cup next to Anwar's seat.

Anwar quickly apologized to the waitress and said, "I'll pay for it."

"Thank you, sir," the waitress replied. We then left the restaurant, saying we needed to return to the hostel before six o'clock.

"Oh, allow me to drop you off at the hostel. You're already my daughter-in-law," Anwar's father insisted.

"No, uncle," Linsha responded, rushing towards the escalator. But Ameena Zubair called Linsha's name. She approached Linsha and held her face in her hands.

"We've given Anwar all our love, care, and attention. Among other things, you are the most beautiful gift I can give him. Mashallah bless" Ameena said affectionately.

Linsha looked sympathetically at Anwar, who gave her a teary-eyed smile. Then she turned to us and said, "Let's go," and walked away, with us following her.

CHAPTER ELEVEN

During the Onam holiday, Linsha and I had planned to return home to Kochi. Her parents arrived from Sharjah two days ago. We were waiting outside the hostel for her dad to pick us up. Eventually, an Innova pulled up, with Baaqir driving and Linsha's father in the front seat.

"Hello, Dad," Linsha greeted her father, but he appeared unhappy and remained silent, making a gloomy expression.

"He's a bit upset," Baaqir whispered to Linsha.

We loaded our belongings into the car and got inside, with Baaqir at the wheel. For a while, we all sat in silence, but then Linsha broke it.

"How's Dubai, Dad? I haven't been there in a long time," Linsha asked, but her father didn't respond. Baaqir glanced at Linsha through the rearview mirror.

"What's wrong, Dad?" Linsha inquired.

"You are the reason I'm not speaking," Raees replied.

"How so, Dad?" Linsha asked.

"Linsha, you've rejected this marriage proposal for a trivial reason," Raees exclaimed.

"A trivial reason? My passion is trivial to you?" Linsha questioned.

"You can continue your business after marriage; Anwar has offered to support you," Raees stated.

"Did Baaqir tell you everything?" Linsha asked angrily, glaring at Baaqir.

"Never mind what he said; their family is wonderful, and you've immediately turned down the marriage proposal," Raees remarked.

"Dad, you just don't get it. You never make an effort to understand," Linsha said.

"Then explain it to me, so I can understand," Raees challenged.

"Dad, Priya and I want to start our own business. I don't want Anwar to foot the bill."

"Whether he wants to fund your business or not, that's his decision. Because they are a respected family, Linsha, you won't receive such marriage proposals again. Stop being stubborn."

"She doesn't have to get married now if she doesn't want to, Dad," Baaqir interjected.

"Baaqir, stop talking; you're still a child. You don't fully grasp all of this yet," Raees said.

Upon hearing this, Linsha burst into laughter.

"Is this amusing to you, Linsha?" Raees asked.

"Dad, did you come all the way from Dubai just to yell at me about this?" Linsha questioned.

"Your life is what concerns me, Linsha. You're wasting it on trivial things."

"Whatever," Linsha mumbled.

After two hours of silence, we finally arrived home. I said goodbye to them and went home with my belongings. When Linsha and her dad entered their home, I could tell that they were not happy. I went home after that.

That night, we were watching a TV movie with my dad when my mother approached me, showing me a picture on her phone.

"Who is this, Amma?" I asked.

"Someone from a matrimonial site sent a request. He's a software engineer named Rajesh," my mother explained.

"He looks nice," I said.

"Should we talk to him? Do you want to call him to arrange a meeting?"

"Mom, I don't mind at all," I replied, albeit somewhat hesitantly. One of my dreams had always been to find someone to marry. How could I refuse a marriage proposal when he reminded me of Vijay

Devarakonda? I admired all of his films, especially 'Arjun Reddy,' where he played a kind character, albeit a bit hot-headed.

"What? You accepted the marriage proposal?" The next morning, Linsha yelled while we were talking in my room.

I retorted, "Shush, you're hurting my ears."

"What about our business, then?" Linsha asked.

"After my marriage, we still have time to pursue it, don't we?"

"Do you really think your future husband will allow it?"

"If he doesn't, then I won't do it."

"What?"

"You know my lifelong dreams, and they've always included marriage over business." I showed Linsha Rajesh's photo. "Look at him; he looks so much like Vijay Devarakonda."

"You and your obsession with Arjun Reddy, the most toxic movie I've ever seen."

"Toxic to you, but love to me."

Linsha's phone chimed with a notification, and I grabbed it.

"Hey, Anwar is messaging you," I said.

"I know, I'm just choosing to ignore it," Linsha replied.

"Don't be rude, Linsha; just talk to him," and I started reading his message. The message read, "I need to talk. How about another meeting?"

"Nice, he's persistent," and I handed Linsha's phone back to her.

"It doesn't seem like persistence. Linsha, he's still interested in you. Why not just give him a chance?"

"It's not about giving him a chance, Priya. Everything will change as soon as I get married."

"You're overthinking it; trust me. Go out with Anwar. Send him a message saying you'd like to meet. Spend some time with him for a day and see if you both connect. If it doesn't work out, then don't proceed."

"But still..."

"Nothing," I said, taking her phone and texting him. Despite Linsha's attempts to reclaim it, I managed to get it.

I wrote on her phone, "I'd like to meet you for a day; after that, we'll decide about our marriage." Then I pressed the "send" button.

"Please, don't do it," Linsha said before grabbing her phone back.

"Linsha, don't overthink it; follow your heart. If you want to go, just press 'send.' Otherwise, don't click. The choice is yours," I said.

Linsha was initially inclined to press

the 'exit' button, but eventually, she seemed unsure. After some time, she sighed and clicked the "send" button. When I took the phone again, I could see Anwar typing.

"Hey Linsha, Anwar is typing something," I said.

Anwar's message came through, "How about tomorrow?"

After showing Linsha the message, I asked, "What should I reply?"

After thinking for a moment, Linsha said, "Send 'Okay.'"

I quickly sent 'Okay.' Anwar responded with a cheerful face and heart emojis.

"Good luck, Linsha; don't mess anything up," I advised.

Linsha let out a bewildered sigh.

CHAPTER TWELVE

Linsha appeared dreadful for the date in her pants and a full-sleeved shirt.

"What the hell are you wearing?" I asked

"Doesn't it look beautiful, though?" Linsha enquired.

"It appears horrible." I took her by the hand and led her inside. I started rummaging through her clothes in search of a worthy outfit in her wardrobe. I found a stunning blue lace dress. I seized it

"This is going to be ideal for you." I said

"Isn't that a touch too much?" Linsha enquired

I told her, walking out and shutting the door to her room, "Go wear it; it's wonderful."

After some time of waiting outside, Linsha beckoned me inside. I entered her room and was in awe. She was stunning in her attire.

"Linsha, you've grown incredibly hot, " I said.

"Well, do you think that meeting Anwar is a good idea?" Linsha enquired

I replied, "It's a great idea, what are you going to do when you meet him?"

Linsha replied, "I don't know."

"Tell me an assumption, though."

"I'll accompany him to a restaurant."

"Then?"

"I'll place a food order."

"Is that it?"

"Is there anything more I need to take care of?"

"Idiot," I called her, and I headed to her wardrobe to retrieve a dress.

"Why are you looking through the wardrobe for dresses?" Linsha enquired

I said, "I'm coming with you."

"You coming with me? I'm meant to go somewhere alone with Anwar, right?" As Linsha said

"Yes, but you'll mess everything - EVERYTHING -if I don't go with you." After saying that, I gave her a pair of Bluetooth earphones to wear.

"Hear what I'm saying with these headphones, ok?" I said

"Is it necessary?" questioned Linsha.

"Yes, it does," I replied as I changed into new clothing.

"Where is he? It has been thirty minutes." At one of the al fresco restaurant (outdoor restaurant) tables where Linsha was seated, I questioned her through the Bluetooth earpiece from a distance while also peering at her to give her instructions. I was sitting outside on a cast iron bench close to the garden, far away from her, and I could see her from where I was sitting.

"Let's give him a some more time." Linsha said through her earphones.

"Oh my lovely Linsha, are you not crying as you wait for him?" I joked when I said it.

"Shut up, please." She answered and then shushed me, "Shhh, He is coming."

Despite being too far away to see him, I managed to peep.

"Yes, I noticed him. Anwar , I saw him." I said

"Now that he is coming towards me, what should I do?" Through her earphones, Linsha whispered softly to me.

"Boys often adore a lovely, giggling face on girls with moving hair behind the ear. Do it," I said and then i pleaded "please dont ruin anything for god sake".

Anwar started opening his mouth after seeing her , so Linsha grinned at him.

"Hey fool, shut your mouth." I can hear a masculine voice behind me saying it, and right then, I saw Anwar closing his mouth. At that precise moment, I heard the same guy behind me say, "Say you look so beautiful to her."

"You look really beautiful today," Anwar said, which I overheard via my headphones.

I found it odd, so I turned around and glanced back. I noticed a man using headphones and speaking to someone. He was Rajesh, so I walked up to him. Rajesh is the same individual who proposed to me on a matrimonial website.

"Hey, you're Rajesh. Isn't it?"I questioned him.

"Priya? matrimonial website?" Rajesh Questioned

"Linsha, wait a moment. I'll get back to." I spoke to Linsha while wearing headphones, and then I removed them. "You spoke to someone, I overheard," I questioned Rajesh.

"I'm assisting a pal with his date over there, but it's a secret." He gestured towards the table in the outdoor restaurant where Anwar and Linsha were seated.

"Anwar? "I asked Rajesh.

"Yes, but how did you know his name?" Asked Rajesh

"Because my buddy Linsha is dating Anwar," I explained, "Even I am assisting her by guiding through headphones."

My headphones started to sway as I heard it, so I quickly put them in.

"Priya, where the fuck are you?" Linsha enquired

"Hello, what happened?" With headphones on, I asked.

"I had trouble expressing myself when I was talking to Anwar. I'm in a bloody bathroom. Where have you been?" Linsha enquired

"I've returned. I'm back now. you go to your table." I said

"Okay," said Linsha. I turned to look at the restaurant. I saw Linsha returning to her table from the lavatory.

I said to Rajesh, "I think we should work together to hook them up."

He extended his hand for a handshake and remarked, "Let's work together." I gave him a handshake.

Actually, Linsha and Anwar were receiving guidance from me and Rajesh on how to make their date successful. We served as the puppet masters and they as thc puppeteers, but Rajesh and I are currently having the actual date. Funny thing is, Linsha and Anwar have no idea that Rajesh and I were working together to mend their relationship.That's how we kept going. They were compelled to ride bikes by Rajesh and myself, Me and Rajesh rode bikes behind them as they began to ride.

The bike ride from Kochin to Palakkad was quite far.

"There is a little mountain close to the Palakkad district, yet it is big enough to give a view of the entire city. " As he was riding the bike, Rajesh told me.

"Is it beautiful?". I asked

"It is, indeed." Rajesh said

"Through headphones, tell Anwar about it. "I said

"Hello, Anwar listen to what I say. Tell Linsha about a mountain close to the district of Palakkad. It is the most romantic place." I heard Rajesh speaking through the headphones.

"Hey Linsha, there's a mountain close to Pallakad district," Anwar replicated the same line that Rajesh said. "There is a really beautiful place."

I whispered into my headphones, "Tell let's go," to Linsha.

"Let's go now," Linsha said to Anwar.

We all arrived there after a short while. It was an enormous mountain.

"What should I do right now?" Rajesh was questioned by Anwar over the headphones.

"Climb the mountain by grasping Linsha's hand." Rajesh informed him.

Anwar and Linsha began climbing the mountain.

"Hold my hand, and come with me." Rajesh insisted me. I began to climb while still holding his hand.

"Hurry up! Before the sunset, we need to reach the summit." Rajesh informed me

I questioned, "Why?"

"Wait and watch." Rakesh stated. We continued to ascent.

We finally reached the top after an arduous climb.

"Anwar, now cover Linsha's eyes. Until I say so, do not open." Anwar was told by Rajesh over headphones. After that, Rajesh covered my eyes with his hand.

"What are you doing?" i asked to Rajesh

"Just wait " Rajesh replied.

Rajesh covered my eyes for a bit. Rajesh began the countdown.

Rajesh urged Anwar through the headphones, "3.....2.....1.....hey Anwar, open Linsha's eyes," and Anwar simultaneously moved his arm away from her eyes and Rajesh moved his arm away from mine. When I opened my eyes and witnessed the most stunning sunset of my life, I immediately felt magnificent. I've always observed sunsets from the surface of the sea, but I've never witnessed one underneath an urban area. Blue and orange were among the many colours that painted the sky. It was exquisite.

I whirled around to face Rajesh and gazed into his eyes.

Through his headphones, Rajesh instructed Anwar to repeat after him whenever he say.

"It was one of my dreams to have you here.—the most gorgeous girl in the most gorgeous place—made this moment even more lovely. To be with you, to care for you, to gaze into your eyes every single minute and feel as though I have something valuable in my palm that I can feel the affection, the adoration, the fixation, and the love on you—these are all things I want to always have with me. I want you to be with me every day and night......always." These beautiful words were spoken to me by Rajesh while he held my hands; Anwar simultaneously spoke the same words to Linsha. I was really close to rajesh. it felt like, We felt an attraction from some unseen thrust. My own heartbeat could be heard in addition to his. I caressed his cheek with my fingertips. He moved closer, and I was hypnotised by the enchantment in his eyes, so I couldn't help but kiss him on the lips.

We kissed, stared into one another's eyes, then I whirled to look at Linsha and Anwar. We could still see how passionately they were kissing. They straight away kissed each other vigorously without waiting for our instructions. I then sprinted in their direction in an effort to humorously ruin the situation. Upon seeing Rajesh and I together, they were both surprised. For Linsha and I, it was the friendliest and most romantic day ever.

This is Linsha and my first experience riding with boys late at night, and it's now quite late. Back to Kochin, where we currently live. I was sitting behind Rajesh while he was riding the bike, embracing him so firmly that I thought it was the most comfortable thing I've ever experienced. Anwar was riding the bike with Linsha sitting behind him. I wished that the journey go on forever.

We finally arrived at my and Linsha's home after an amazing three-hour ride. Raees, Linsha's father, had a dejected expression as he stood in front of the home. After dismounting the bike, Linsha went meticulously in the direction of the home. Raees walked towards Anwar with his arms tied behind him.

"In my heart, I've already accepted you as my son-in-law, even though as a father I shouldn't be approving these acts. The marriage between you and my daughter will be discussed when I call your father. " While grinning, Raees said

Anwar blushed and replied, "Thank you, uncle."

I turned and saw Linsha. After grinning, She went into her home..

"When we first met Anwar at Nimsha's wedding, he was flirting with Linsha," I asked Rajesh about it, "If he was very good at that, why did you bother to help him today?"

"He believed that girls preferred flirting over talking, although this is untrue. Actually, that might have been the primary factor in Linsha's initial rejection of his marriage proposal. So I assisted him," Rajesh remarked.

"Playboy, huh?" I joked.

"You can refer to me as a 'love guru'."

I said, "We both officially become 'love gurus'," and we both chuckled. Rajesh then turned to look at his watch.

"Damn, it's too late." Rajesh turned to Anwar and said," Hey, Anwar, it's time to go."

To Rajesh, Anwar waved.

Rajesh remarked as he turned towards me. “gotta go, Goodnight."

I held his cheek in my arm and drew him into a kiss. I said “Goodnight.” Rajesh grinned at me. He mounted the bike and rode off. I kept a passionate gaze on him as he rode away.

CHAPTER THIRTEEN

Present day (Dr Arnab's Narration)

"I married Rajesh on February 2, 2018, the same day Linsha and Anwar exchanged vows. It marked the first time a Hindu-Muslim wedding took place in the same hall. Linsha had her nikkah in the same venue while I tied the knot at the Guruvayoor Temple. Following my wedding, we all gathered at the same reception hall," Priya explained.

After finishing her story, Priya headed to her room, retrieved their wedding album from the cabinet, and returned to show us.

As I noticed a Hindu family and a Muslim family taking a group photo together, it filled me with delight. This sight made me realise that Priya and Linsha's relationship transcended societal biases.

"This group photo of you all is truly beautiful," I remarked.

"It's one of our favourite memories. Rajesh and I have had our share of disagreements since we got married. There are aspects of our personalities that don't always align. However, Anwar and Linsha never seemed to have conflicts. They used to post several entertaining reels on Instagram, most of which were humorous. I'd often giggle while watching them, wishing Rajesh and I could do something similar. We taught them about love, but they taught us how to keep our love alive, where we fell short," Priya said, her tone tinged with sadness.

Sensing her melancholy, I decided to change the topic.

"Tell me more about your company. Is it still operational?" I inquired.

"That's one of the most challenging chapters in our lives," Priya replied.

"Why is that?" I asked.

"We took out a loan to start the company, and due to our lack of experience, we overspent on advertising and other expenses. Initially, everything went smoothly, but just before the COVID lockdown, we landed a major project. We invested a significant amount in decorative items, but the lockdown spelled disaster for our venture. We had to repay over 2 crore rupees," Priya revealed.

"2 crores? That's a substantial amount," I exclaimed.

"Yes, we did manage to repay it eventually," Priya confirmed.

"How did you both come up with such a large sum of money?" I probed.

"I sold the jewelry my parents gave me for our wedding, which fetched between 25 and 30 lakhs. After Anwar's death, Linsha contributed the majority of the funds. Anwar's business also suffered due to the COVID lockdown, and he was unable to provide any financial support. I have no idea how Linsha managed to cover everything," Priya explained.

"So, Linsha single-handedly paid over Rs. 1 crore?" I clarified.

"Yes, that's correct. She gave up everything for the business, even her unborn child. She had an abortion due to her dedication to the business, with her husband's approval. I was initially shocked and even despised her for it," Priya admitted.

"That's unusual," I remarked.

"I'm sorry?" Priya inquired.

"Nothing, it's just a surprise. What was the name of your company?" I asked.

"BONNY INTERIORS - A Place to Live," Priya replied.

"That's a catchy name. Where was the office located?" I inquired.

"Thrissur, not far from Kuriachira," Priya answered.

After checking my watch, I stood up. "It was a pleasure meeting you, Priya, but it's getting late," I said, extending my hand for a shake. Priya shook my hand.

"I appreciate you letting me relive those wonderful memories," Priya said.

"It must be bittersweet," I remarked. "I wish I had experienced such times. Anyway, we should get going. Goodbye."

She smiled and replied, "Goodbye."

Greeshma, Ankhitha, and I left her house. I started the car once we were inside. Greeshma sat in the back seat, while Ankhitha sat next to me, and we began to drive.

"I thought Linsha killed Anwar due to their strained relationship, but Priya's story suggests something different," Ankhitha commented.

"It's quite an intriguing and remarkable love story," Greeshma added.

"Yeah, hearing her tale gave me goosebumps," Ankhitha said.

Then Greeshma turned to me and asked, "Why are you so quiet? Don't you want to address Priya's claims in any way?"

"We need to pick up Basi from LuLu Mall, right? Give him a call," I said.

"Oh, I forgot about that guy. Let me call him," Ankhitha said, dialling his number. Basi ignored the call and hung up.

"He's not answering," Ankhitha informed us.

"Let's grab a quick meal at LuLu Mall then. KFC okay with everyone?" I suggested.

"Yes, I'm hungry too. Let's go," Greeshma exclaimed.

"She's the ultimate foodie," Ankhitha teased.

"And I'm proud of it," Greeshma replied.

I parked at LuLu Mall, and we headed to the food court on the third floor, where various dining options were available, including KFC and Pizza Hut.

"Greeshma, which one do you prefer?" I asked.

"KFC, of course!" Greeshma enthusiastically replied as she headed towards KFC.

"Her love for food knows no bounds," Ankhitha commented.

"While you can't cure an obsession, you can manage it. There must be a way to keep it under control," I said.

"How?" Ankhitha inquired.

"You'll see soon," I replied, making my way to the KFC restaurant.

Greeshma placed her order with the waitress: "A 16-piece bucket, extra crispy chicken, spicy or Kentucky grilled, KFC's Mashed Potatoes and Gravy as a side, and a 1-liter bottle of Pepsi."

"Is there anything else you'd like, ma'am?" the waitress asked.

"What else is left to order? She practically bought the entire restaurant," I joked, and the waitress chuckled.

"Thank you for the order," the waitress said before heading to the kitchen.

"I've never heard of some of these delicacies before Greeshma placed the order," I remarked.

"Stick with me, Doctor, and you'll explore a world of culinary delights," Greeshma teased.

"Doctor, be careful; you might transform from a muscular hot body into a chubby one," Ankhitha warned.

Greeshma playfully glared at Ankhitha. "A hot body with muscles, huh?"

Ankhitha blushed but then noticed someone standing behind me and pointed, saying, "Hey, isn't that Basi?"

When I turned around, I saw Basi with a girl. I was surprised when I recognised her and exclaimed, "Hey, that's my sister Gayathry. What's she doing with Basi?"

Ankhitha and I got up and walked over to them. Gayathry glared at me and froze when she saw me.

"What are you doing with Basi here, Gayathry?" I asked in a brotherly tone.

"Chettayi, what's Ankhitha doing here with you?" Gayathry countered.

“Gayathry, please answer my question first," I insisted.

"We're just friends, Arnab," Basi explained.

Gayathry shot Basi a scornful look and said, "No, Chettayi, he's my boyfriend."

I was taken aback, and Ankhitha seemed equally surprised.

"Boyfriend? What are you saying, Gayathry?" I questioned.

"We've both been in relationships, Chettayi," Gayathry said.

"It's a bit much for me to digest, I'm sorry. I'm heading out," Ankhitha said as she walked toward Greeshma. Greeshma looked dejected upon seeing Basi with Gayathry and rushed to the restroom with teary eyes.

"She's just a friend of mine, Arnab," Basi insisted.

"Oh! So you really intended to end our relationship?" Gayathry asked Basi.

"Yes, I did," Basi admitted.

"Hello, I'm still here," I interjected.

"Chettayi, he's leaving me; he doesn't understand how much I love him," Gayathry said, her voice breaking.

I gave Basi a disapproving look, and he hung his head in shame. I approached Gayathry while she waited by the elevator. I reached out and held her shoulders when I saw her crying.

"So you came here with friends, huh?" I teased.

Gayathry managed to smile through her tears.

"You shouldn't have kept it from me; our relationship is more like that of best friends than brother and sister," I said.

"Basi told me two days ago that he wanted to end our relationship, Chettayi. I didn't have a chance to talk to you about it," Gayathry explained.

"So your trip from Thrissur to Kochi was to meet Basi?" I inquired.

"With a guilty smile, Gayathry replied, "Yes, Chettayi."

"How did you know he would be traveling with us?" I asked.

"He said he was going on a trip with his friends, so I had no idea you'd be there too. I didn't know the Ankhitha he mentioned would turn out to be your friend," Gayathry said.

"Are you hungry?" I asked.

"To be honest, I am," Gayathry admitted.

"Let's have a meal then," I said, putting my arm around her shoulder as we walked back to the KFC restaurant.

We all sat at the same table. Basi looked embarrassed, Gayathry ate while giving Basi angry glares, Ankhitha and I exchanged uncomfortable glances, and Greeshma appeared dejected.

After dinner, we decided to head back home. We all returned to the car, with Basi, Gayathry, and Greeshma in the back seat, and Ankhitha in the front. I started the engine, and there was silence in the car for a while. To break the ice, I decided to bring up the topic of Linsha.

"Ankhitha, you asked for my opinion on Priya's story about Linsha," I began.

"Yes, what do you think?" Ankhitha inquired.

"I'm not sure why, but ever since Priya mentioned that Linsha had to repay a debt of over one crore, it's been on my mind," I said.

"Do you think this issue is related to the motive behind the murder?" Ankhitha asked.

"People often resort to drastic measures when they have no other options. Linsha has made sacrifices for her company before, including having an abortion to help it grow. Her business has always been her top priority," I explained.

"So, what could Linsha possibly gain from murdering her husband?" Gayathry asked.

"Maybe money. After her husband's death, she immediately repaid her loan," I replied.

"She could have just asked him for it. Why resort to murder?" Gayathry wondered.

"Priya mentioned that Anwar's business was also in jeopardy due to the COVID lockdown," I said.

"Yeah, this lockdown caused a lot of hardship for many people," Gayathry acknowledged.

"People sometimes do desperate things when they're struggling due to lack of resources. That could be a reason," I added.

"A murder's motive could also involve a broken heart," Gayathry remarked, causing a tense moment. I exchanged a somewhat angry glance with her.

"Oh, great! Now she wants to kill me," Basi quipped.

"You've hurt me deeply," Gayathry retorted.

"I warned you that our relationship wouldn't work," Basi stated.

"Why did you suddenly decide we couldn't be together? Give me an explanation," Gayathry demanded.

"You won't understand," Basi replied.

Their argument continued, and Ankhitha and I exchanged irritated looks.

"I shouldn't have brought up this topic," I whispered to Ankhitha.

"You're right," Ankhitha agreed.

Gayathry and Basi kept arguing, so I turned up the radio volume to drown them out. Glancing into the rearview mirror, I noticed that Greeshma still appeared to be in a gloomy mood.

I dropped off Basi, Greeshma, and Ankhitha at Skyline Flat.

"So, what's next?" Ankhitha asked.

"We need to find out more about her company," I replied.

"How?" Ankhitha inquired.

I smiled and said, "Let's figure it out."

"How about meeting for coffee tomorrow?" Ankhitha suggested.

"At 4:00 PM, after my duty?" I proposed.

"At Café Coffee Day?" Ankhitha confirmed.

"At Café Coffee Day, indeed," I agreed.

After that, Ankhitha left for her flat. I smiled as I watched her go. Then, with my sister Gayathry in the car, I drove home.

CHAPTER FOURTEEN

When we arrived home, our father was waiting for us in the yard.

"Molee, I was worried about you. How did you two end up back together?" he asked.

"She was with her friends, and I was with mine, so we happened to be in the same place at the same time," I explained.

"That's good. It annoyed me when your mother questioned why I allowed you to go out alone," Dad said.

"When Chetayi goes out alone, you don't worry, but you're always concerned when I hang out by myself," Gayathry protested vehemently.

"Molee, you're a girl; of course, we'll worry," Dad replied.

"Why should girls have to endure such double standards?" Gayathry muttered as she entered her room.

Dad turned to me and asked, "What happened to her?"

"Acha, you don't need to worry. She had a disagreement with her friends. I'll handle it," I assured him. I then headed for her room and rang her doorbell.

"May I come in?" I asked.

"No, just leave," Gayathry replied, her voice shaky.

I entered her room and sat down on a chair.

"You know, I've always thought of you as my best buddy, but you've always treated me like a chetayi. All I wanted was for us to have a close sibling relationship, not for you to see me as a little sister who needs to be afraid of her big brother. I feel like I failed in some way," I said, trying to emotionally persuade her to share her love story. I got up and started to leave the room.

"Chettayi..." Gayathry's gentle voice called out, and I turned to look at her.

I smiled at her as I met her gaze.

"Basi... we first chatted through Instagram. He was so funny that I couldn't stop talking to him," Gayathry began.

"Yeah, he's a bit of a character," I said.

"That's what I like about him. You know how much I love fictional stories, Chettayi. Basi used to share his own made-up stories with me. Some were romantic, some were mysteries or crime stories, and so on."

"So, you connected with him through your shared interests?"

"Yes," Gayathry replied.

"Who made the first romantic proposal?" I asked.

"He was the one who proposed, and I'll never forget that day."

"What happened on that day?"

"He had set up a room with colorful decorations, balloons, and flowers. But the most adorable thing was a giant portrait of me made from flowers. He did it all by himself. I remember how he proposed, and I was touched by his effort. I just swiped at his feet."

"That's beautiful. So why does he want to end things now?"

"Chetayi, I don't know. We've had occasional disagreements and clashes, but isn't that normal in any relationship?"

"Maybe some people just can't handle issues; they run away. Your mother used to call such people 'boneless fellows,'" I said, and we both chuckled.

"Our relationship faced many challenges due to the typical intercaste issues once his parents found out. He left his home to be with me for several years. That's why he now lives in that apartment. He used to have strong feelings for me, but I can't understand why he decided to end our relationship. Lately, he's been finding comfort in someone else, perhaps because he has grown too attached to Greeshma," Gayathry confessed.

"Ankhitha mentioned that he lives with his mother," I responded in surprise.

"What? He's a deceitful person. He lied to manipulate my feelings. He's an arrogant womanizer," Gayathry exclaimed in anger.

I interrupted abruptly, seeing her getting consumed by rage. "It's late, time to go to bed," I said before turning to leave.

She called me "Chettayii."

"Yeah?"

"Can you talk to Basi about this? Please try to resolve the issue. He's someone I truly love, and I can't just forget about him," Gayathry pleaded passionately.

I understood the complexity of female emotions, especially when it comes to love, so I assured her, "I'll try," before saying good night and closing the door.

CHAPTER FIFTEEN

My first day back at work was exciting, but now it feels routine. Something is missing. Two o'clock has already passed, and I'm still waiting. My mind keeps going back to the wonderful time I spent with Ankhitha the day before. I feel an urge to see her right away. I still have two more hours to finish my work, but it feels like an eternity. Time is passing so slowly. After what seems like an eternity, my phone finally flashes 4:00 p.m. I rush to my car, start it, and drive to Cafe Coffee. There, Ankhitha is already waiting for me.

I ask, "You got here early."

"Just five minutes," Ankhitha replies.

I take a seat and say, "Let's order something." The waitress comes over.

"Sir, yes?" she asks.

"A cappuccino and..." I look at Ankhitha.

"Please, a hot cocoa," Ankhitha tells the waitress.

"Alright, anything else?" the waitress asks.

"Nothing," I say. I was about to start a playful conversation when Ankhitha interrupts.

"So, what's our next move?" Ankhitha asks abruptly. It's clear that her main concern right now is getting to the bottom of the murder case.

"We need to find out more about Linsha's business," I continue, sighing.

"How?" Ankhitha asks.

"I did some online research last night and found out everything I could about her company. Now that I have the address, we can go there."

"But how will going there help us learn more?"

"They've rented space in a commercial complex for their office. I found the owner's phone number online. Let's call and make an appointment."

"Okay, let's get started, hurry."

"Let me finish this coffee first, please."

"Oh, I forgot about that," Ankhitha says. I can tell she's completely focused on this case.

"You keep thinking about that murder, don't you?" I ask.

"Yes, I do. It was the worst day of my life. I couldn't save him, and he died. The guilt will always haunt me. Getting justice for him is the least I can do."

"Don't let this incident weigh on your mind. He didn't die because of anything you did. Sometimes, in dire situations, we're unable to save lives. You can call it fate or destiny, but no one can change the fixed times," I reassure her.

She falls silent for a moment and sheds a few tears.

"Let's visit her office and inquire about Linsha and her company at nearby stores," I suggest. Ankhitha brightens up at the idea.

She smiles and gives me a look as we continue to discuss our plan.

The upper floors of the building housed an office with a sign that read 'Bonny Interiors,' but it appeared to be closed and covered in dust. Downstairs, there was a home painting shop, and I went in with Ankhitha. An elderly man, possibly in his 70s, was working as the shopkeeper, wearing a blue shirt, black pants, and glasses.

I asked the shopkeeper, "When will BONNY INTERIORS open?"

The shopkeeper gave me a puzzled look, adjusted his glasses, and approached me.

"Who are you?" he inquired.

"Well, I'm a doctor, and I came here to discuss a contract for them to decorate the interior of my house," I lied, hoping to get some information about what had transpired with the business.

"That business was founded by two young women, right? They thought they could outdo Mukesh Ambani," he said, chuckling.

"What happened to them?" I asked.

"You should have seen how they launched the business. They planned events, invited a celebrity, and did who knows what else for publicity. They were regularly and arrogantly misbehaving, and those girls were foolish."

"So the business permanently closed down?"

"Of course, they borrowed money from the bank, and when they couldn't repay it, the bank seized the property. Additionally, they wouldn't have taken a loan from Pramaan if they were smart, but they weren't."

"Who is this Pramaan?"

"Pramaan is a ruthless person. He lends money at 20% interest and then launders black money through the petrol station business. Pramaan and those two girls got into a lot of trouble. They were publicly humiliated as he shouted at them. The girls were caught up in this mess during the COVID lockdown."

"How much harassment did these women endure? That's excessive."

"Why did they put in all this effort in vain? They ruined everything because of this. Women shouldn't be doing all of this; they should get married as soon as possible and serve their husbands. And Pramaan even threatened to kill them."

I quickly said, "Thank you for the information, uncle," and noticed Ankhitha's anger. I held onto her hand and whispered, "Let's go, come on."

We walked back to the car, and Ankhitha was still visibly upset.

"It frustrates me that everyone here always wants to elevate men above women," Ankhitha said.

"Just ignore them; they're ignorant," I replied.

"I really want to give that guy a piece of my mind."

"Hey, calm down."

"Idiots," Ankhitha muttered, her anger still simmering.

"Have you noticed something about the people here? They're narrow-minded. That might have been one of the reasons this company failed."

"Narrow-minded?"

"I mean they have a limited mindset that believes men should always be superior to women, just like he claimed."

"True, maybe the COVID issue wasn't the only reason her company failed."

"Yes, Linsha was under immense pressure to repay the money. We need to meet this Pramaan guy. Get back in the car," I instructed. After getting Pramaan's address from the shopkeeper, I joined Ankhitha in the car, ready to move forward with our investigation.

The building resembled a palace, and a sign that read "Pramaan's Palace" adorned the gate in a grand manner. This person had amassed an enormous amount of money by offering loans to numerous people without authorisation. As Ankhitha and I arrived, I noticed an elderly man sitting on a deck chair, chewing paan, dressed in a white cotton dhoti without an uppercloth.

"HEYY HEYYY HEYY, who are you people?" the elderly man yelled.

"I'm here to meet Mr. Pramaan," I replied.

"Oh, my boy, PRAMAAAAAAN," the elderly man shouted, spitting out the paan while doing so. Ankhitha looked quite alarmed.

"Don't make that face," I whispered to her, and she abruptly looked away.

A bald, obese man in a blue shirt and brown trousers opened the front door.

"I'm Pramaan; how may I help you?" he asked.

"I want to inquire about Linsha and Priya," I said calmly.

"Oh, those two bitches," the elderly man yelled.

"What specifically would you like to know about those bitches?" Pramaan inquired.

While I was taken aback by the derogatory terms used to refer to Linsha and Priya, I refrained from commenting on it, as my primary goal was to gather information about why their business had failed. So, I fabricated a story to learn more.

"I learned about Linsha's business failure when my brother received a marriage proposal from her. I've come here to find out more about her," I explained.

"OH! Do you know that bitch is already married?" the elderly man exclaimed.

"Her husband died," Pramaan added.

"That bitch killed him for his insurance money; otherwise, how could she repay such a large sum? Her damn business went down the drain," the elderly man claimed.

I was shocked by these allegations and asked, "Wait... wait... wait. How did you find out about that? The insurance, tell me about it."

"Anyone who takes my money as a loan, I completely distrust. I have a friend who used to work at a Bajaj insurance company. He told me," Pramaan explained.

“We could have lowered the repayment on that bitch's loan if I had asked her to sleep with me. Instead of hitting me, that cocky bitch slapped me.” the elderly man said.

This time, I started to get angry, but i managed to restrain myself by tightening my fist.

"Can I speak with your acquaintance who used to work for Bajaj Insurance Company? I need more information about her. It concerns my brother's life," I said.

"Here's his number, 8075640968," Pramaan replied, giving me the contact details.

I copied the number into my phone and saved it in my contacts.

"I appreciate your help," I said to Pramaan.

"There's a ripe banana over there," I mentioned, pointing to the elderly man.

"Where?" The elderly man turned around.

"It's rotten, so there's not much use for it. It's an entirely ruined old banana, so even if you want to eat it, you can't," I said as I turned away. Ankhitha suppressed a giggle as we both walked towards the gate.

"I didn't understand what he was saying," the elderly man said in an odd manner.

"You've lost your ability to move, so stay still. Why don't you just age and die already?" Pramaan remarked before heading inside.

"What a place," Ankhitha said as soon as we were in the car.

"He certainly is. What a charmer!" I commented.

"But I enjoyed your banana reference. I wish I could have laughed right then," Ankhitha said, chuckling.

"At least, we did learn something here," I said.

"About the insurance?"

"Yes, it might have played a role in Linsha's decision to kill her husband."

"Everyone wants a loving husband. According to Priya, Anwar and Linsha got along great. Linsha's obsession with this business has ruined everything."

"It's okay to be passionate about something, but when it turns into an obsession, terrible things can happen."

"So, what's next?"

"I'll drop you off at home. It's already 6."

Ankhitha replied in a somber tone, "Yes, of course."

"You need to stop thinking about this case for today and give your mind a break. You're becoming consumed by it," I advised as I started the car.

CHAPTER SIXTEEN

I was in Ankhitha's room, and she had prepared three freshly made juices for us. Greeshma was looking dejectedly at Basi, who was engrossed in his phone. Ankhitha distributed the juices to each of us.

"Give this a try, Doctor," Ankhitha said as she handed me a glass.

I took a sip and asked, "Is this pineapple juice with ginger?"

"Yes, it is. How does it taste?" Ankhitha inquired.

"It's good," I replied.

"It's disgusting," Basi chimed in, clearly trying to annoy Ankhitha. In response, Ankhitha playfully threw a pillow at him, causing juice to splatter on his face.

"Just so you know, the bathroom is that way," Greeshma chuckled, pointing towards the restroom. Basi, with a disgruntled look, got up and headed towards the bathroom. As soon as he left, the rest of us burst into laughter.

"So, what's your theory about Linsha's case? What more information do you guys have about her?" Greeshma inquired.

"In my opinion, she's driven by a strong desire for money," Ankhitha remarked.

"Based on my assessment of Linsha's personality, she seems highly focused on establishing a successful business. Priya, on the other hand, may not have shared the same level of enthusiasm. Linsha's over-investment is probably why they took out a loan," I explained.

"But why would she resort to killing her husband?" Greeshma wondered.

"According to Pramaan, Anwar had a life insurance policy for Linsha, and the COVID situation also spelled trouble for Anwar's business. Linsha might have felt she had no choice but to obtain the funds, and her last resort could have been Anwar's life insurance policy," I said.

When Basi returned from the bathroom, his clothes were damp from the juice. Ankhitha couldn't help but laugh when she saw him.

"That might be the motive, then," Greeshma commented.

"Perhaps, but we need concrete evidence to prove it. We'll need phone records or social media chats at the very least," I pointed out.

"I might be able to help you guys," Basi said.

"You can help?" Ankhitha asked.

"I'm skilled at hacking WhatsApp IDs," Basi claimed.

"Really? Do you even know how to turn on a computer?" Ankhitha teased.

"Please, I can make pineapple juice more efficiently than you," Basi retorted.

"Settle down, you two. Do you actually know how to hack?" I inquired.

"The only information I need to quickly hack someone is their IP address or their phone number if they have an Instagram account linked to it," Basi explained.

"Where did you learn all this?" Ankhitha asked.

"Naturally, from YouTube," Basi replied.

"Can you do it right away?" I asked.

"I'll need at least a day. Maybe I can have it fully hacked by tomorrow," Basi said.

"Do it," I said.

"It's not free, guys. I want something in return," Basi said.

"What do you want?" Greeshma asked.

"Each of you needs to pay 500 rupees," Basi said.

"He's joking, as I expected," Ankhitha said.

"I'm serious," Basi insisted.

"Just do it, Basi. I'll give you a thousand rupees if you want," I offered.

"Okay, send me the Instagram accounts on WhatsApp. Tomorrow, I'll hack them and give you the information," Basi said.

I shared the Instagram IDs of Linsha, her brother Baaqir, and her parents through WhatsApp using my phone. The timestamp on my phone indicated that it was 8:30 p.m.

"Oh, it's 8:30. I have to leave. Ankhitha, please come with me," I said, and Ankhitha followed me as I headed out. When we reached the elevator, I pressed the down button.

"Have you noticed that Greeshma has been looking downcast lately?" I asked Ankhitha.

"Yes, she seemed upset after we left LuLu Mall," Ankhitha said.

"Do you remember when you visited my house, and you asked me why I was annoying my mom? I explained the concept of 'cute aggression' to you," I said.

"Yes, and I even Googled it as you suggested," Ankhitha replied.

"Have you noticed that Greeshma often playfully bites and pinches Basi? She's like acting aggressively but in a cute way towards him."

"Friends often tease each other like that," Ankhitha remarked.

"But Greeshma has a soft spot for Basi, which is why whenever she goes out, she always brings his favorite sandwich with her. She doesn't bring anything for you; it's always for Basi," I explained.

"Doctor, what are you getting at?" Ankhitha asked.

"Greeshma is in love with Basi. That's why she's been feeling down. She also has a complex about her weight. Instead of letting her mind spiral into jealousy, just talk to her and console her," I suggested.

The elevator doors opened, and I stepped inside. Ankhitha looked somewhat astonished.

"Take care of her," I advised before the elevator doors closed.

CHAPTER SEVENTEEN

The phone in my cabin rang, and I picked it up. The receptionist on the line informed me about the appointments for the day.

"Are there any appointments today?" I asked.

"We have two appointments scheduled, but there's also someone here without an appointment, claiming to be Basi," the receptionist replied.

"Oh, I know him. Please send him in," I said.

"Alright, sir," the receptionist replied and hung up.

Basi entered my cabin shortly after.

"Hey, Basi, what brings you here?" I asked.

"I thought I should drop this off to you while I was passing by," Basi said, holding up a pendrive.

"A pendrive?" I inquired.

"Yes, there's software on it. Once you install it on your computer, the username and password will appear. I wrote them down in a notepad and saved them on the pendrive. After logging in, you'll have full access to Linsha, Baaqir, and their parents' Instagram IDs," Basi explained.

"You hacked it, impressive," I said, surprised.

"Yeah, but where's my 1,000 bucks?" Basi asked.

I chuckled, took my wallet out, and handed him 1,000 rupees, saying, "Here you go."

"I'm going to use it to buy my favourite dress," Basi remarked as he got up.

"Wait a second; I'd like to talk to you," I said.

"What now?" Basi asked impatiently.

"I want to discuss Gayathry with you," I said.

Basi remained silent for a moment, his expression somber.

"I don't know what the issue is between you two or why you want to break up with my sister. If there's a problem with your parents regarding your relationship with Gayathry, I can talk to your parents about it." I offered.

"No, Doctor, that's not it," Basi replied.

"So what is the problem?" I inquired.

"I know Gayathry is upset right now, but she needs to understand that our relationship won't last," Basi sighed. "We're going to break up sooner or later. It's better for us to part ways before it's too late. I know I'm hurting her, but it's necessary," he added before turning and leaving.

For a moment, I was left puzzled by his situation. It seemed like he had some hidden issues or concerns he wasn't willing to discuss. It might have something to do with the ongoing love triangle involving Basi, Greeshma, and Gayathry. I figured they needed to sort it out amongst themselves.

I then connected the pendrive to my laptop, installed the software with the provided password, and gained access to Linsha's phone. I could now see her phone screen in real-time. Basi was indeed a hacking genius.

While I was working on this, Ankhitha called me on the phone. I answered her call.

"Yes, Ankhitha?" I said into the phone.

"Are you busy right now?" Ankhitha asked.

"What's going on?" I inquired.

"Greeshma is indeed in love with Basi, just as you suspected," Ankhitha confirmed.

"I warned you," I replied.

"What should I do? She's really upset right now. When I asked her about it, she started crying," Ankhitha said.

"Don't worry; she'll be alright. I promise," I reassured her.

"Can you talk to her in person?"

"Right now?"

"Anytime. We're going to Zelex Mall. Can you meet us there?"

"I'll be there at 3:30, alright?" I agreed.

"Thank you so much, Doctor. We'll see you there," Ankhitha said before ending the call.

Greeshma, Ankhitha, and I were sitting in the Waffle Cafe. Greeshma seemed upset, and she wasn't eating. I joined them at the table.

"Am I on time?" I asked.

"No, Doctor, you're right on time," Ankhitha rcplied. I turned my attention to Greeshma, who appeared to be holding back her emotions.

"Hello, Greeshma..." I began, but she cut me off.

"I know what you want to talk about, but I don't want to," Greeshma said, her voice shaky as she started to cry. We sat in silence for a moment because I was at a loss for words. Then, I had an idea to help her overcome her depression and gain some perspective on her situation.

"When was the last time both of you bought dresses?" I asked.

"Not recently, at least," Ankhitha answered.

"Come on, get up; let's go buy some clothes for both of you," I said, and they followed me as we headed to Max's clothing store.

Inside the store, there was a wide selection of clothing on display. "I want Greeshma to do something for me," I said.

"Why?" Greeshma asked, clearly annoyed.

"Please, just do it for me," I pleaded.

"Tell me what it is!" Greeshma demanded.

"You have to pick and try on a variety of dresses from different fashion categories. Don't check the size or style, just gather them and try them on. However, once you've picked them, you can't go back and get more. You can only choose from the dresses you've gathered," I explained.

"Doctor, are you insane?" Greeshma protested.

"I'm serious," I said, "and I'll buy you a Pepperoni pizza if you do it." Greeshma initially hesitated, then turned to Ankhitha.

"Just do it for me," Ankhitha said with a sweet smile. Greeshma sighed and reluctantly agreed.

"Fine," Greeshma said, "I'll do it."

"Great, now gather a variety of clothes without checking the size," I instructed.

"I GOT IT, DOCTOR!" Greeshma exclaimed.

"What's the purpose of making her do this?" Ankhitha asked.

"People sometimes need to experience things to truly understand them," I replied. Greeshma started gathering clothes.

"Collect different styles, don't worry about the size," I reminded her.

"I UNDERSTAND, DOCTOR," Greeshma said.

Greeshma gathered the clothes and asked "What do I do now?"

"Now, you wear them," I replied.

"Right now?"

"Yes," I said.

Greeshma let out a loud "AAHHH" and entered the dressing room. After a while, she unlocked the door and emerged wearing a green churidar that fit her perfectly.

"It looks good in terms of size, but I don't like the colour," Greeshma said.

"But the size is right," I noted.

"I didn't like it, though," Greeshma insisted.

"Alright, try another one," I suggested. Greeshma closed the door to try on another dress. She emerged wearing a crimson sheath dress.

"I liked it, but it's too small," Greeshma said.

"Yes, the size is off," I acknowledged.

"But the design is beautiful, and I think I can find a larger size," Greeshma said.

"No, you can't," I replied. "Remember, it's a random selection."

"Do as he says, Greeshma," Ankhitha encouraged.

"Alright," Greeshma agreed, "I'll try another one." She returned to the dressing room.

Greeshma tried on more than ten dresses, some of which she didn't like, and some were the wrong size. At one point, she became frustrated and did this reluctantly. Finally, she tried on a stunning red dropped waist dress that had the perfect pattern and size.

"Do you like it?" I asked.

"I love it!" Greeshma exclaimed.

"Greeshma, you look stunning in it," Ankhitha added.

"Thank you," Greeshma said with a smile.

"But I'm still confused. Why did you make her do this?" Ankhitha asked me.

"She needs to realise that Basi isn't worth it," I replied. Greeshma turned to me and scowled angrily.

"Why did you put me through all this?" Greeshma demanded.

"You tried on many dresses, some of which were the right size for you, but you didn't like them, and some you loved and preferred, but they didn't fit. Just like how some people may like you, but you have the choice to accept or reject them. Love is strong when both people choose to be together, just like how the red dropped waist dress and you were a perfect match, and you looked beautiful in it," I explained.

Greeshma smiled at me, tears in her eyes. "Someone better is waiting for you," I said, placing a hand on her shoulder. "You just have to wait, okay?"

"Okay, Doctor, let me change back into my clothes now," Greeshma said, closing the dressing room door.

"I saw her smile, even though it was a bit forced. I appreciate it a lot. But couldn't you have just told her instead of making her try on ten dresses?" Ankhitha asked.

"People don't always accept things just by hearing them; their minds can remain fixed on the problem. By having them experience something different, it takes their focus away, and they can then listen to what I have to say more clearly," I explained. I noticed Ankhitha's puzzled expression. "It's a bit hard to explain, so let's leave it at that," I said. Ankhitha laughed when she heard that.

While we were in the clothing store, a woman with a red dot on her forehead and wearing a maroon saree walked by. Ankhitha noticed her and immediately hid.

"Why are you hiding?" I asked Ankhitha.

"That's Gowri Pakash; I told you about her, the troublemaker in our apartment," Ankhitha explained.

"Oh, the one who spreads rumours," I recalled.

"Yes, her."

"Do you think she can help us now?"

"Why do you need her help?"

"Let's inquire about Linsha immediately."

"Are you insane? She'll start spreading rumours about us having an affair to everyone."

"Just follow my lead, don't worry." We both approached Gowri.

"Hey there, Ankhitha, how's your mental health?" Gowri asked Ankhitha.

"Better than yours, aunty," Ankhitha replied. Gowri then turned to me.

"Who's this handsome guy, Ankhitha? Your new partner?" Gowri teased.

"Why bother?" Ankhitha retorted.

"You're a feisty one, little devil," Gowri said.

"Do you know Linsha, who lives in 8th B?" I asked.

"Linsha... Yes, she talks to Ashwarya often at the playground," Gowri replied.

"Who is Ashwarya?" I inquired.

"I don't know much about her, but Linsha and she were often seen together," Gowri said.

"Have you noticed anything strange about Linsha?" I asked.

"Why, handsome boy, is Linsha your latest crush?" Gowri teased.

"Please answer his question; it's important," Ankhitha urged.

"How would I know?" Gowri responded.

"Doctor, forget it; she's just a waste of time," Ankhitha said.

"Doctor?" Gowri questioned skeptically.

"Yes, he's a psychologist," Ankhitha informed her.

"You poor girl, I was right. Did you really lose it?" Gowri said.

"Yes, I did. Any issues?" Ankhitha retorted.

"Be careful, mole," Gowri warned. "Hey, I remember something about Linsha," she added after a moment.

"What is it?" Ankhitha asked.

"As I was heading up to the 8th floor, I heard an argument coming from 8th B. It sounded like a young guy was yelling at a woman," Gowri recalled.

"Do you remember what they were talking about?" I asked.

"The young guy was begging for money, and she was refusing to give it to him. He also mentioned something about helping her cover up a crime, but she still refused to give him the money. They were yelling about something related to her husband's insurance," Gowri explained.

"Did you see their faces?" I inquired.

"I didn't see their faces, but the woman kept calling his name. It sounded like something starting with 'Baa...'" Gowri said.

"Could it be Baaqir?" I asked.

"Yes, that's it, Baaqir," Gowri confirmed.

"Thank you for the information," I said.

"Why do you need all this information?" Gowri asked.

"It's not your concern," Ankhitha replied, and we quickly made our way to Greeshma, who was finishing up trying on dresses.

"That woman again, oh my god," Greeshma sighed when she saw Gowri.

"Don't worry; we're leaving," I assured her. We rushed to the cashier to pay for Greeshma's chosen outfit.

"The bloodthirsty Gowri Prakash will undoubtedly fabricate lies about me and Dr.," Ankhitha commented as we sat inside a cafe.

"Why did you approach her?" Greeshma asked.

"Ask him; he wanted to talk to her about Linsha," Ankhitha replied.

"Gouri actually gave us some very crucial information," I explained.

"Don't completely believe her. Every story she creates, she always adds some seasoning," Greeshma warned.

"At least 20% of it could be genuine," I suggested.

"How will you determine the 20% truth?" Greeshma asked.

"She brought up the subject of life insurance. How does she know about that?" I questioned.

"Oh yeah, she did," Ankhitha realised.

"How did she find out?" Greeshma inquired.

"She used one of her go-to tactics: eavesdropping on Linsha and Baaqir's conversation outside Linsha's flat," Ankhitha explained.

"She went on to say that Baaqir had told Linsha about how he helped her cover up her crimes and asked for money, but Linsha had refused to pay," I added.

"So, do you think Baaqir is involved in this crime?" Ankhitha asked.

"When we first met Linsha, I told you that based on her body language, she didn't seem like someone who could cover up crimes. I believe her brother took charge of cleaning up her mess," I said.

"So, we'll go after her brother next," Ankhitha suggested.

"Yes. But I need to know more about him. He's a student pursuing an MBBS degree at Anpal Medical College. That's where we'll start," I explained.

"What can we find out about him there?" Greeshma questioned.

"We all spent the majority of our time in college and at school when we were students. His teachers and friends, among others, can shed light on his personality. There's no doubt we'll find something," I said.

"So let's hope there's something for us to discover there. This time, Gouri Prakash used her foul tongue to impart essential information," Ankhitha remarked, and we all laughed at her scathing comment.

CHAPTER EIGHTEEN

Unable to fall asleep due to the sound of the rain and lightning outside, I was startled when my laptop chimed. I got up and checked my laptop to find some fresh WhatsApp conversations in Linsha's and Baaqir's accounts, which Basi had hacked for me. I began reading through the messages, and while many of them were common, like meme videos and family discussions, I noticed a specific chat history between Baaqir and Linsha when I searched for "insurance" in the WhatsApp search panel. This chat history was four months old.

Baaqir: Better pass over the money now.

Linsha: I don't have it.

Baaqir: I need the money right away; it's urgent.

Linsha: Why are you in such a rush? For your bloodied marijuana?

Baaqir: How dare you speak to me in such a manner. Remember that I was the one who covered up your crime. Aren't you having fun with your husband's insurance money? Give me a little of that.

Linsha: I'm done now. You won't get it from me.

Baaqir: Fucking bitch.

Linsha: Watch your tongue. If I can kill my husband with no second thoughts, I can kill you too. Don't mess with me; I'm telling you.

I read through the conversation and then reviewed it again. However, there were no other conversations like this. It seemed like an outburst between them in the heat of an argument. I decided to print their chat history on paper. At the same time, I made up my mind to visit Baaqir's college the next day to gain a better understanding of his character.

"This is how a medical college seems, then," Ankhitha remarked as we arrived at Anpal Medical College.

"Ambulances, lots of young adults in white coats. This is unmistakably how a medical school looks," I responded.

"How do we start?" Ankhitha asked.

"Let's begin by entering some random department, maybe the microbiology section, and ask a quick question about Baaqir to the teacher on duty," I suggested.

We approached a young woman in a white coat who was passing by.

"Excuse me, could you direct us to the microbiology section?" I inquired.

"Follow me. I'm actually headed there," she responded.

"Do you know a student named Baaqir?" I asked as we walked alongside her.

"I can't recall any Baaqir. What batch is he in?" she inquired.

"His batch is 2016," I replied.

"Oh, I don't know anyone from the 2016 batch. Although I'm not in close contact with them, I have met some. I'm from the 2021 batch," she said.

"Alright, thank you," I said as we continued to follow her. We headed to the college's first floor.

Before I could express my gratitude, the girl exclaimed, "Here we are," and hurried into a classroom. We then proceeded to the microbiology department.

"May I come in, Professor?" I asked upon entering the HOD's office. The professor, who had a bald head and round glasses, allowed us entry.

"I'd like to learn more about my nephew, Baaqir," I said, claiming to be his local guardian.

"Oh, regarding his curriculum?" the professor inquired.

"More about his performance here," I clarified.

“Alright, let me call one of the junior faculty members because they are the ones who handle that,” the professor said, ringing a bell. A junior professor stepped out of her office. She was dressed in a green churidar and a white coat and appeared to be in her thirties.

"Yes, sir?" the junior professor asked.

"Meet Dr. Vaishnavi," the professor introduced her.

“Hello, madam,” I greeted her.

"Please provide him with the information he’s requesting; he is Baaqir’s local guardian," the professor instructed.

"Baaqir? Which batch?” Dr. Vaishnavi inquired.

“He is from the 2016 batch,” I replied.

"Oh, yes! Raees? I know him. Baaqir Raees, right?" Dr. Vaishnavi asked.

“Yes, that’s him,” I confirmed.

"The most apathetic student I’ve ever come across. He failed three times in his second year. I don’t understand why he even enrolled in this course. He doesn’t attend classes, do any assignments, or even show up for exams. He consistently fails,” Dr. Vaishnavi explained.

"Does he have any positive qualities? Is he intelligent?” I inquired.

“Intelligence couldn’t be attributed to him. I regret to say that he’s the most academically challenged student I’ve encountered,” Dr. Vaishnavi replied.

I thanked them for the information and exited the office with Ankhitha.

“Are you sure that this Baaqir was involved in hiding Linsha’s crime?” Ankhitha asked with a smile.

"We can’t draw conclusions based on just one person’s perspective," I replied.

We visited other departments and inquired about Baaqir. Everyone had a similar opinion of him, describing him as a terrible student. Baaqir seemed to be a classic underachiever according to their accounts. However, in the pharmacology department, we encountered a young professor who stood out from the rest. He was dressed casually in jeans and a t-shirt, and he had long, straight hair. Unlike the other teachers, he seemed to be very friendly with students, so I decided to approach him.

"My name is Dr. Arnab, and I'm Baaqir's guardian," I introduced myself.

"Dr. Arnab? Guardian?" the professor questioned with some caution.

"My name was listed as the second guardian on his admission forms," I explained, lying deliberately.

"Oh, I see. I'm Ravi, the pharmacology professor," he introduced himself.

"I came here to inquire about Baaqir's performance. Everyone seems to agree that he's a terrible student," I said with a chuckle.

"Baaqir? What batch?" Ravi asked.

"He's from the 2016 batch," I replied.

"Oh, I know him well. He's a slacker but the most brilliant student I've ever seen," Ravi stated.

"Brilliant? That's quite the opposite of what I've heard from other teachers," I said.

"Those teachers only appreciate students who complete assignments, attend classes regularly, and submit their tests on time. They focus on rote memorisation. Baaqir is different. He engages deeply with the subject matter when it's presented clearly to him. He doesn't study just to pass exams; he genuinely wants to learn. I can recall being pleasantly surprised when he asked me a question," Ravi explained.

"What was the question?" I asked.

"The question was related to the opioid chapter. We were discussing enkephalins and endorphins, which are two opioid-like substances in the human brain. Typically, they're only produced when needed. We all know that opioids give us a pleasurable feeling. So, his question was, 'Does the motivation we get from another person release opioids, giving us that pleasure? Does this explain why the counselling section in psychiatry always prevails?'"

"That's quite an intriguing question," I remarked.

“However, he cannot be accepted by our for-profit educational system, which is primarily concerned with grades, revenue, and marketing. In actuality, Baaqir is a very intelligent guy. When he sees any scientific subjects in the films he watches, he questions me about them. ‘Suspect X,’ a Korean film, and ‘7th Day,’ a Malayalam film, were two recent viewings for him. He keeps raising concerns about that movie.”

“What sort of questions?”

“The themes of both films revolve with forensic loopholes and dead body swiping. Whenever he asks me a serious question, he occasionally drives me insane.”

“Dead body swiping? That’s intriguing.”

“Both fascinating and annoying. But I applaud all of his attempts to convey his ambiguity. He will undoubtedly make a discovery at some point that will change how we all live in the future.”

"Professor, I appreciate your time,” I said.

"You shouldn’t be concerned about him. I’ll handle him; after all, it was my tutelage that helped him achieve decent grades in forensics and pharmacology.”

"Wow! I appreciate that as well,” I replied before leaving with Ankhitha to make our way to the canteen.

“What are your thoughts about Baaqir, Dr.?” Ankhitha questioned, but I was lost in thought and didn’t respond. Ankhitha had to raise her voice to get my attention, saying, "HELLO!"

"Yes, indeed," I responded, snapping back to reality.

“What are you contemplating?” Ankhitha inquired.

“Baaqir’s questioning regarding dead body swiping has me stumped,” I admitted.

“But I didn’t quite get that part,” Ankhitha confessed.

“There is no doubt about Baaqir’s depth of expertise in forensics and pharmacology,” I explained.

Ankhitha asked, “So?"

“It mentions in the newspaper that Anwar had an accident the day after your birthday, so keep it in mind,” I reminded her.

“Yes, it explains why I‘m still puzzled,” Ankhitha acknowledged.

"Because Baaqir is aware of the flaws that can alter forensic evidence. He managed to make the murder case look like a vehicle accident. We need to find out how he did that."

"How? Three years ago, the matter was already adjudicated as an accident."

"As far as I know, autopsies are also performed in accident cases. First, we must obtain the autopsy report."

"How will you acquire it?"

"Let's try; one of my friends is a police officer. He's stationed in Palakkad."

"Okay," Ankhitha said with a sigh. "I'm confused about a particular thing, why did the other teachers disparage Baaqir?"

"Teachers often blame the students to cover up their own shortcomings. Nowadays, education, especially in the medical field, is a source of pride. People don't care about the teacher's work; they just want their kids to get admitted to medical colleges to brag about it. Students are intimidated by teachers who threaten to reduce their grades if they complain. Finding good teachers is difficult for the management because they're more focused on marketing and profit. Although imparting knowledge is the true purpose of education, many individuals now view education as a source of pride."

"That's true," Ankhitha agreed with a chuckle. "What's next, then?"

"Let's travel to Palakkad, where Baaqir staged the accident," I suggested

CHAPTER NINETEEN

"So, how are things going, Doctor?" Ankhitha inquired.

"Finally, you've found the time to ask about me," I chuckled and said as I drove.

"As a doctor, you're making a significant contribution to help me solve this matter. May I know why?" Ankhitha asked.

"I'm sure you've seen my interview. Through this case, I believe I can gain a better understanding of what I'm searching for."

"Arnab?" Ankhitha gave me an attentive gaze and inquired, "What are you really looking for?"

"A key to understanding a person's mental state before they commit a crime."

"Do you think that mental illnesses play a role in all criminal activities?"

"We can't label it as an illness. I believe that certain situations, such as mental stress, greed, pride, and the need to survive, drive people to commit crimes."

"Linsha was greedy in this case."

"She was under immense pressure to repay the money, too. She wasn't ungrateful; rather, she was anxious in that terrible circumstance. People can act despicably in desperate times."

"She has already committed the crime."

"She did indeed. Furthermore, by holding her accountable under the law, she should serve as an example for others about the consequences of their actions."

"Yes, she needs to be punished," added Ankhitha. I continued driving, and Ankhitha eventually turned to look at me with skepticism.

"Can I ask you a question, Doctor?" Ankhitha inquired.

"Yes," I said. "Go ahead."

"Have you ever had a girlfriend?"

When she asked that, I was briefly taken aback. "Nope... not yet," I responded, giving her a concerned look.

"Why? You're a doctor, and you're attractive. Girls would surely be interested in you," Ankhitha said.

I chuckled and replied, "In my dreams."

"You've never been in a relationship?"

"In fact, I have."

"Really? Tell me the story."

"The story itself is quite childish."

"Why childish?"

"I've never seen her."

"Really? Without meeting someone in person, how can you love her?"

"Although it may sound cliché, we never actually met face-to-face. We communicated solely through Facebook."

"Arnab, in what year did you chat with her?"

"I think it was 12 years ago. Her username was 'Rockin Lin,' which I can still recall."

"Rockin Lin?" Ankhitha inquired, sounding surprised.

"Yes, why are you surprised?" I asked.

"No... Nothing. What happened next?"

"I was in Abu Dhabi at the time. We were supposed to meet at Al Wahda Mall, but she didn't show up. She never came online after that. She simply disappeared."

"What was her real name?"

"That part was funny. We were unaware of each other's real names. I used the username 'Assassin' on Facebook."

Ankhitha remained silent for a brief moment. She didn't say anything. Then I asked, "What happened? Why the silence?"

"I was curious about how you could still remember her without knowing her name and face," Ankhitha inquired, sounding surprised. "How is that memory still fresh in someone's mind?"

"Because that was my first love, I suppose. Even though the relationship was solely on social media. Facebook was becoming extremely popular around that time. I was also young. We fell in love through the messages we exchanged," I explained.

"Cute but silly."

As I looked at her, I asked, "Are you currently dating anyone?"

"Nope."

"Have you ever dated anyone?"

"No," Ankhitha answered with a dejected sigh.

I noticed she had an unpleasant past from the way she spoke. Perhaps that is one of the factors affecting her relationship with her mom. I decided not to dwell on it further. While I was driving, I turned on the radio.

I greeted my old friend, SI Rahman, who was stationed at the Palakkad police station, as I entered his cabin. He was impeccably dressed in his police uniform, sporting a gunslinging mustache and his hair neatly styled in the typical officer look. Ankhitha, who had never been to a police station before, looked visibly apprehensive.

"Hey, Inspector Rahman," I said.

Rahman got up from his chair and inquired, "Where have you been, Doctor?"

"Brother, I've been quite busy lately," I replied.

Rahman then turned his attention to Ankhitha and asked, "Who is she? Are you two dating?"

"Watch what you're saying, Mister. She's my friend," I clarified.

Rahman grinned menacingly but motioned for us to take a seat.

"Arnab, what brings you here?" Rahman inquired.

"Actually, Ankhitha witnessed a murder," I explained.

Rahman gave Ankhitha a cold, distrustful look, which made her uneasy.

"Don't worry; I was joking," I reassured her with a laugh after noticing her expression.

"Stop joking. What do you really want?" Rahman pressed.

"Actually, I'm curious to learn more about a three-year-old car accident case," I stated.

Rahman raised an eyebrow. "Three years ago?"

"Yep. The incident occurred in Palakkad. The records should still be here, right?"

"It should be accessible. But I do need to know why you're asking. If you don't inform me, I won't be able to help," Rahman responded sternly.

Recognizing Rahman's commitment to honesty, I had no choice but to share everything we had been investigating, including what Ankhitha had witnessed and Linsha's entire story.

"Are you certain Ankhitha actually saw the murder?" Rahman inquired.

"You know me well enough to know that I won't make any claims without good reason," I assured him.

"When did the accident occur?" Rahman asked.

"According to the newspaper report, it happened on July 20, 2020."

"Let me check it," Rahman said and called over a constable.

Rahman instructed the constable to go to the record room and retrieve the accident report. We waited for a while before finally finding the file. I took it and started examining it. Inside, there were numerous photos of the wrecked car, with a large branch of a tree protruding through the front windshield, causing fatal head injuries to the person who had died. The statement indicated that Anwar had checked into Komaram Lodge on July 19, 2020. When I examined the autopsy report, it revealed that the death occurred between 3 and 4 AM on July 20, 2020. The report detailed several injuries, including chest compression, various leg and hand fractures, rib fractures, and sacral fractures. The head's fragmentation was listed as the cause of death. Tragically, the body was unrecognisable.

"Is DNA testing not performed in accident cases?" I inquired.

"Normally, DNA testing isn't conducted if family members can identify the body. That's what happened in this case. They typically conduct a blood group test to confirm if it matches Anwar's blood group," Rahman explained.

"That's why he kept bringing up the Malayalam film '7th Day' with the lecturer. It was to exploit this forensic loophole," I said.

"What loophole? '7th Day'? Lecturer? What are you talking about?" Rahman asked.

"I visited Baaqir's college to learn more about his personality. One of the professors mentioned that he frequently inquired about forensic weaknesses and body identification methods. I suspect he manipulated the body and dressed it in Anwar's clothing," I explained.

"Are you suggesting that the body we found wasn't Anwar's?" Rahman questioned.

"I believe so. The head was shattered and unrecognisable. It's an irreconcilable body," I stated.

"But how did he acquire a dead body so quickly?" Rahman inquired.

"If you're available, please accompany us to the hotel where Anwar stayed so we can learn more," I suggested.

"I'm free now; let's go," Rahman agreed.

When we arrived at the Komaram hotel, both the police file report and the newspaper article indicated that Anwar had checked in at 6 a.m. on July 20, 2020. Ankhitha, Rahman, and I entered the hotel, which had a somewhat rundown appearance, lacked CCTV cameras, and lacked computerisation. In the lobby, there was an elderly man with a bald head and thick glasses. Rahman approached the front desk.

"I am a police officer. Do you keep records or any proof of the clients?" Rahman asked, displaying his badge. "I'm here to investigate a person who stayed here three years ago."

"Officer, yes. What's the issue?" The receptionist inquired.

"Do as I tell you," Rahman ordered sternly. The receptionist hurried to the nearby cabinet and began searching for the 2020 logbook.

Rahman asked, "Which date and month, sir?"

"It's July, right?" Rahman turned to me.

"July 20, 2020," I replied. The receptionist opened the book and started flipping through the pages.

"For how long have you been working here?" Rahman asked.

"I've been here for eight years, sir," the receptionist replied, and then he found the specific page. "Anwar Zubair checked in at the time indicated on the document, which was July 19, 2020, at 6 a.m." The page had a photocopied copy of an Aadhaar card.

"Are you certain that this is the same person who stayed here?" I asked the receptionist.

"How can I remember, sir, when it's been years? It could be the same person if I received it from the man with the Aadhaar card," the receptionist explained.

"People wore masks back then because it was during the COVID era," I mentioned.

"Oh yes! People were wearing masks back then, and I prohibited them from removing them," the receptionist recalled.

"They could have provided a fake Aadhaar card, so you should have checked their faces," Rahman scolded him in a police-like manner.

"That suggests that the person who stayed here might be Baaqir," I speculated.

"That's a possibility," Rahman agreed.

"I have a suspicion," I asked both the receptionist and Rahman simultaneously, "Is there a mortuary nearby?"

"Oh yes, there's a government hospital two blocks away," the receptionist informed us.

"Thank you. Let's go," I ordered. Rahman, Ankhitha, and I headed for the car that had brought us there. I drove, with Rahman sitting next to me and Ankhitha in the back seat.

"Why are we going to the mortuary?" Ankhitha asked.

"I believe Baaqir took the corpse from the mortuary," I explained.

"How could a body be taken in such a manner?" Rahman inquired.

"He mentioned the Malayalam film '7th Day' as his inspiration. Let's go there to find out how he pulled it off," I said and drove to the mortuary. It was located behind the government hospital, and a security officer was dozing off in his chair. Rahman woke him up.

"Are you sleeping on duty?" Rahman questioned him.

"Who are you to give me orders?" The security guard responded impolitely.

"I'm a police officer," Rahman declared, displaying his badge.

The security officer was taken aback, stood up awkwardly, and introduced himself as Ravi.

"Mr. Ravi, you're always sleeping, so it's no wonder dead bodies are disappearing from this place," Rahman scolded him sternly.

"Missing dead bodies, sir? Who told you that? No bodies are being sold here," the security guard hesitated but then admitted.

"I haven't mentioned selling. Do you actually sell dead bodies here?" Rahman asked him firmly.

The security guard stammered, "No, no, sir."

"Are you familiar with Baaqir?" I inquired.

"Who is Baaqir?" The security guard asked. I showed him a picture of Baaqir that I had downloaded from Instagram on my phone. "Did this guy buy a corpse from here?"

When the security guard saw Baaqir's picture, he became visibly frightened and stammered, "I don't, I don't know..."

We could tell he was lying, so Rahman slapped him, grabbed his collar, and threatened him. "I'm going to kick you so hard in the genitals that you won't be able to urinate properly if you don't confess. What happened? Tell me."

Terrified, the security guard finally said, "Don't do anything, sir; I'll tell you everything."

"Tell us everything," Rahman ordered firmly.

"I've seen him around here occasionally. He once paid me 80,000 rupees to take a body from here," the security guard admitted.

"If the body disappears, wouldn't their family inquire?" I asked.

"Most of the bodies brought here are unidentified. They might be homeless individuals. Some of them we donate to medical schools," the security guard explained.

"So Baaqir paid you the money and took a body, is that correct?" Rahman confirmed.

"Yes, that's the man who gave me the money. I don't know his name," the security guard replied.

"Do you remember the date?" I inquired.

"I'm not sure of the exact date, but it was years ago," the security guard said.

"Stay here; you'll do anything for money. I'm calling a couple of police officers to take you to the police station," Rahman said after the security guard pleaded with him not to press charges. Rahman handcuffed him.

"The whole thing is confusing me," Ankhitha said. "What happened that day?"

"I've pieced together what happened that day in my mind. Baaqir is a genius and a criminal," I explained.

"Could you please elaborate? I'm also baffled," Rahman requested.

I turned to face Ankhitha and began to explain the sequence of events. "Linsha murdered Anwar on July 19, 2020, around 2:00 a.m. You witnessed it and sought your father to call the security officer. Both of you headed to block B. Anwar's body was taken by Baaqir, who likely placed it in the vehicle, possibly in the trunk, and drove away toward the main entrance. The security guard wasn't present to record the car's license plate in the logbook as an exit because he was preoccupied with you in block B. To establish an alibi that Anwar had stayed at the Komaram hotel, Baaqir later traveled to Palakkad, used Anwar's Aadhaar card, and checked in there. Baaqir wore a mask to hide his face from the hotel clerk. Afterward, he concealed Anwar's body in a hidden location. To retrieve a dead body, he went to the mortuary. The security guard at the mortuary mentioned that Baaqir used to come there occasionally. Thus,

Baaqir was likely aware of the illegal sale of bodies taking place there. He then collected the unidentified body that may have been involved in the accident case on July 20, 2020. Baaqir dressed this body in Anwar's clothes, placed Anwar's wallet, driver's license, and Aadhaar card in the vehicle, and positioned the body in Anwar's driver's seat. He orchestrated the accident in some way."

"Consequently, based on the blood group matching Anwar's, along with his driver's license and Aadhaar card, we assumed that the body we found at the accident scene belonged to Anwar," Rahman expressed his amazement - he concluded.

"Indeed, it's just like the plots in '7th Day' and 'Suspect X.'"

Ankhitha inquired, "But why did he go to the trouble of removing a body from the mortuary?"

I explained, "To manipulate the time of death in an autopsy report. Remember what Linsha told us when we first met her? She claimed that on July 20th, she was shopping at a grocery store. If we review the CCTV footage of that location, she can easily prove that she wasn't in Palakkad at the time of the accident."

Ankhitha expressed her disbelief, saying, "I can't believe these criminals, both the sister and the brother."

I turned to Rahman and implored, "Rahman, I need your help now. How can we prove all of this in court?"

Rahman explained, "This happened three years ago, and it's a challenging case."

I asked if there was no way to prove it, to which Rahman replied, "There is only one possibility. If your theory is correct, we need to gather some circumstantial evidence so that the court can order exhumation."

Ankhitha inquired about exhumation, and Rahman explained, "Exhumation is the process of digging up a deceased person's body from their grave. Since Anwar was a Muslim, he would have been buried. To conduct a DNA test and compare it with the body that was buried, we need a court order. If Arnab's theory is correct, the buried body won't match Anwar's DNA."

I then asked what if Linsha confessed, and Rahman wanted to know how we would make her confess.

I replied, "We need to use our wits and take action."

Rahman agreed, saying, "It's a clever move. We also need to compile the life insurance policy claim records to determine Linsha's motive for the murder. Additionally, the security guard at the mortuary needs to serve as a witness who saw Baaqir retrieving the dead body, and we have Ankhitha as an eyewitness to the murder. All of this is necessary to prove the crime, and if we can do that, the court can order exhumation."

I nodded and said, "This seems to be the only way to prove that Linsha murdered Anwar. So let's do it."

CHAPTER TWENTY

After two days, Rahman and I met at Ankhitha's flat to discuss our plan.

"So, here's the strategy: Since the case was already closed, we can't simply reopen it. Therefore, we need to contact Anwar's parents and ask them to file a complaint expressing doubts about Anwar's death. Then, even though it's against the law, we can summon Linsha and Baaqir for questioning and press her to confess," Rahman explained.

"Actually, that's an excellent plan. If something goes wrong, we can argue that we summoned Linsha and Baaqir in response to Anwar's parents' complaint," I added.

"However, there's a potential issue. If things go awry, Anwar's parents might be accused of a false crime. According to Section 211 of the Indian Penal Code, anyone who initiates or causes a false criminal process or falsely accuses someone of an offence can be held accountable," Rahman pointed out.

"Oh my God, that's risky, isn't it?" Ankhitha exclaimed, looking concerned.

"The security guard confessed that Baaqir had taken a body from the mortuary, so it's clear that he's involved," I said.

"Yes, I warned the security guard that I could press charges against his family if he lied in court," Rahman stated.

"Was that really necessary?" Ankhitha raised an eyebrow and turned to Rahman.

"Lady, you have no idea about this field. I've witnessed many instances where witnesses changed their testimony in court. We always need a backup plan," Rahman explained.

"Have you met the medical professional who conducted Anwar's autopsy?" I inquired.

"I did. He conducts numerous autopsies every day. He couldn't recall the specific case because it occurred three years ago. Nevertheless, we already have the autopsy report; his statement will only be a formality," Rahman replied.

"What about the money from Anwar's life insurance that Linsha claimed? Did you obtain the agency's records?" I asked.

"I did. The bank account number matched Linsha's SBI account. According to the life insurance company's records, she received the funds and deposited them into that account," Rahman confirmed.

"Alright, then. We have the documentation as proof that she indeed received the money," Ankhitha noted.

"Okay, we need to meet with Anwar's parents soon to inform them of everything. Only then can they file a complaint," I concluded.

It was an imposing mansion with three levels, exquisitely adorned. Anwar was undeniably wealthy. Rahman, Ankhitha, and I went to his house and rang the doorbell. The front door swung open, revealing an elderly bald man in a white shirt and grey lungi.

"May I help you?" the elderly man inquired.

"We've come to see Anwar Zubair's parents," I said.

"I am Zubair, Anwar's father," the old man replied.

"We're here to discuss Anwar's death. I'm Inspector Rahman," Rahman introduced himself.

"Anwar's death? He died in an accident," Zubair stated.

"All will be explained to you. Will you allow us inside?" Rahman asked.

Zubair looked puzzled but motioned for us to enter. Descending the stairs was an elderly woman with a scarf covering her head, dressed in a blue maxi.

"Ikka, who are these people?" the old woman asked.

"He's a police officer," Zubair replied

Rahman asked "And she is?"

"Ameena, my wife," Zubair answered.

"Anwar's mother," Rahman clarified. "We should all take a seat. This concerns the death of your son."

We all sat down on the couch in the entrance hall.

"Officer, I don't understand. Our son died in a car accident. Why this unexpected meeting?" Zubair inquired.

"Mr. Zubair, I need you to stay calm and pay close attention to what I'm about to say. Your son wasn't killed in an accident; he was murdered," Rahman revealed. Ameena's eyes welled up with tears upon hearing this.

"What? Nonsense! Who would kill my son?" Zubair exclaimed.

"We believe Linsha, his wife, murdered him," Rahman stated.

"Linsha? That can't be. She was at her flat when the accident happened," Zubair argued.

"Unfortunately, the car accident did not cause your son's death. He was killed in Linsha's apartment," I added, pointing to Ankhitha. "She is the only eyewitness who saw Linsha striking Anwar with a rod."

"Are you sure, young lady?" Ameena asked, looking at Ankhitha with tears in her eyes.

Upon noticing Ameena's distress, Ankhitha glanced at her and then turned to me. I nodded, indicating for her to explain what she saw.

"I saw a woman using a rod to attack Anwar through the window," Ankhitha explained, noticing Ameena's tears.

"And the accident? What's the story there?" Zubair questioned, his eyes welling up with tears.

"Our thorough investigation revealed that the body we found at the accident scene was not actually Anwar's," I revealed.

"What?" Zubair shouted as he stood up.

"Mr. Zubair, please calm down and remain seated," Rahman urged.

"How can I calm down? It has been three years since my son's death, and we believed he was buried in a cemetery. Now you claim the body we buried wasn't Anwar's?" Zubair said sternly.

"I understand your feelings, Mr. Zubair," Rahman acknowledged.

"Inspector, you don't comprehend the police negligence here," Zubair asserted.

"We made a mistake, Mr. Zubair, and we apologise for it. We are aware now. To help us prove in court that Linsha killed Anwar and to prosecute her, we kindly request your cooperation. So please, calm down," Rahman said.

Upon hearing this, Zubair sobbed and held Ameena, sitting back down. Ameena turned to us with red, teary eyes.

"Why did Linsha kill my son?" Ameena asked angrily.

"We discovered that Linsha had a significant debt to repay. Her lifestyle was extravagant, and we learned that your company had also been temporarily affected by the COVID lockdown. She saw Anwar's life insurance as her last chance to clear her debts," I explained.

"I would have helped her sell my house if she needed the money. How could she kill my son for gain?" Zubair cried.

"I realised she was a deceitful and selfish woman. I have no idea what she did to my son to make him fall," Ameena said.

"Linsha's confession is the key to proving this crime. We need your assistance with that," Rahman said.

"How can we help?" Zubair asked.

"First, you need to file a complaint against Linsha, expressing your suspicions about her involvement in your son's murder. Then, we can summon her for questioning. I will use our methods to get her to confess," Rahman explained.

"Then let's do it," Ameena said to Zubair.

"We will," Zubair agreed.

"Very well, come to our police department tomorrow to file the complaint," Rahman instructed.

CHAPTER TWENTY-ONE

"What's your plan, Rahman?" I inquired as we both parked our vehicles next to Linsha's at the Skyline building after two weeks of surveillance.

"We've been monitoring Linsha's activities for the past two weeks, but we haven't been able to track Baaqir. We have no idea where he is. Additionally, since her parents are in Dubai, they can't file a habeas corpus while we have her in custody," Rahman explained.

"The case would be stronger if both Linsha and Baaqir confess simultaneously," I suggested.

"That's true. The phone number you provided to trace Baaqir is currently unreachable, but don't worry; we'll find him soon."

"I wonder what our plan is for today," I mused.

"Linsha usually goes to the park with her friend Ashwarya every Tuesday," Rahman said.

"Yes, I remember Gouri Prakash mentioning that," I replied.

"Gouri Prakash, who is she?" Rahman inquired.

"She's Ankhitha's neighbour."

"Alright, look over there." Rahman pointed to the building's entrance and said, "She's a lady constable." The constable was dressed in a yellow churidaar.

"She will lure Linsha to come with us. We can discreetly place her in our car and take her to the police station for questioning without attracting attention from the public," Rahman explained.

"I hope everything goes smoothly," I said. We waited for over an hour. Linsha eventually emerged from the lift, wearing a crimson churidaar, and appeared to be chatting happily with the lady constable Rahman had pointed out.

Rahman suddenly exited our vehicle and approached Linsha as she walked towards us.

"We need to question you at our police station, so please cooperate," Rahman informed her, with the lady constable holding Linsha's hand.

In a fearful tone, Linsha asked, "What's going on?"

"We'll discuss it at the police station," Rahman replied. Linsha reached for her phone to make a call, but the female constable swiftly took it from her and escorted her into the police vehicle.

In the interrogation room, Linsha sat trembling, Rahman and I observed her through the glass. Her hands were shaking, and she started to perspire. She appeared genuinely frightened.

I commented, "All we need to do is scare her a bit, and she'll spill the beans."

"Why are you so sure?" Rahman asked.

"Even if she's committed a crime, she doesn't know how to cover her tracks. Just look at her; she's radiating fear. Baaqir was the one coordinating and covering everything up."

"Alright, let's get started," Rahman said, and he entered the interrogation room. Linsha was visibly alarmed and started to cry while trembling. Rahman gave her an intense stare, while I remained behind the glass.

"Since we both know why you're in custody, it's best if you confess because we both know why we detained you. Otherwise, we'll use police methods that you won't be able to withstand," Rahman said.

"I don't understand... officer... Why am I here?" Linsha asked nervously.

"How did you murder Mr. Anwar Zubair?" Rahman inquired.

Linsha whispered trembling, "I didn't murder..."

Rahman suddenly slammed his hand on the table, startling Linsha.

"Don't play games, lady. We have all the evidence," Rahman said as he picked up a file from the table. He showed her Anwar's life insurance claim history. "We know you took out multiple loans. You were only concerned about your business." He then pointed to a WhatsApp conversation I had printed, where Baaqir had messaged her, "How dare you speak to me in such a manner, Remember that I was the one who covered up your crime. Aren't you having fun with your husband's insurance money? Give me a little of that."

"It's clear that you killed your husband for his insurance money. We just need to know how you did it. If you don't want to be dealt with the cop way, we'll make you wish you were never born," Rahman threatened.

Linsha nervously questioned, "How can you accuse me of killing Anwar just based on his life insurance claim history and our loans?"

"Because we have an eyewitness who saw you attacking Anwar with a rod. Linsha, we know about Baaqir's attempts to cover things up, and we know his methods. There's no way out. You should confess," Rahman asserted.

"I'm not telling you anything," Linsha replied fearfully.

"Alright, Baaqir has been apprehended. We'll interrogate him in a more intense manner," Rahman stated as he stood up, moved toward the door, and then came over to me.

"What's the plan?" I asked Rahman.

"We'll scare Baaqir," Rahman said.

"You caught him?"

"No."

"How can you intimidate him then?"

"I'm hoping she'll fall for it when we play a distressing sound through the speaker," Rahman explained. He then played an audio clip on the laptop, connected to the speaker. The audio featured a man's screams after being struck by a rod, and it was agonising to listen to. Even I felt disturbed by the sound.

As soon as Linsha heard it, she started crying, covered her ears in distress, and eventually lost patience, walking over to the glass.

"PLEASE STOP IT, STOP IT. Please stop hurting my brother. I WILL TELL EVERYTHING; I WILL CONFESS," Linsha cried out.

"Yes!" Rahman cut off the audio. He then entered the room where Linsha was being interrogated and began recording her confession on video.

"Please provide details of what happened in your flat on July 19, 2020, at 2:30 a.m.," Rahman requested.

Through tears, Linsha began, "Anwar came to my flat unexpectedly that day. I begged him for money to help pay off my loans, but he couldn't provide the funds due to the COVID situation affecting his business. I was desperate and had to find a way to repay the money. As far as I could remember, Anwar had a life insurance policy. So, I had to get the money. I grabbed a rod from the main hall, hit him with it hard, and then again. When I checked his pulse, he had none. I called my brother Baaqir since I didn't know what to do. When he arrived, he took Anwar's body away and placed it in a large duffle bag. After that, I'm not sure what Baaqir did to cover it up, but he made it look like an accident in some way."

"So you killed Anwar for his insurance money?" Rahman asked.

"I admit that I killed him for his money, with a clear conscience," Linsha declared. Rahman let out a sigh and turned off the camera.

"Lastly, where is Baaqir?" Rahman inquired.

"What? I heard you assaulting Baaqir," Linsha said, astounded.

"That was just a ploy to get you to confess. You genuinely have no idea where he is, do you?" Rahman asked.

"No, I don't," Linsha replied.

Rahman then got up and walked over to the door, turning back to face Linsha. He said, "Women these days struggle to find a decent partner. You had one, but you killed him out of greed. What a waste of a life you are. Prepare to spend the rest of your life in jail."

Rahman then came to me and said, "Mission accomplished. Now we just need to track down Baaqir."

"Something doesn't feel right," I said skeptically.

"What's not right?" Rahman asked.

"It seems like she rehearsed these confessions before admitting to them. She didn't provide many details about the money demand and Anwar's surprise visit."

"Why do you think that?"

"Well, she did mention checking Anwar's pulse, and the details she provided about those events seemed genuine. However, when it comes to the circumstances surrounding the money request and Anwar's surprise visit, she didn't go into as much detail."

"Wow, wow! She confessed, that's what matters. She will be held accountable for her actions regardless."

"Yes, maybe I'm overthinking this. So, how do you plan to locate Baaqir?"

"We're putting everything on the line. Unfortunately, his phone is still untraceable, likely due to dismantling. We can't put Baaqir on the no-fly list or a black mark in train station now because Linsha's confession statement and report haven't been presented to the Magistrate's Court yet. You know how our legal system is unreasonably slow. We need to find him before he leaves the country."

"Let me try it my way. Ankhitha knows a hacker who might be able to help. He's the one who hacked into Linsha and Baaqir's instagram accounts."

"You know that's illegal, right?"

"Don't press charges against him."

"I won't. But he needs to stop these illegal activities after this."

"I'll talk to him about it, I promise. But right now, we need him."

"Carry on then."

"So she confessed?" Ankhitha asked in astonishment while discussing the situation with Greeshma and Basi, who were in Ankhitha's apartment with me.

"Yes, she did. Now all that's left is to track down Baaqir," I confirmed.

"Can't the police just locate him?" Greeshma inquired.

"It's a bit complicated. Rahman has just submitted Linsha's confession to the magistrate's court. According to Rahman, there are still some legal requirements to fulfill before they can put Baaqir on the watchlist," I explained. Then, I turned to Basi and said, "Basi, I need your help."

"Me? What can I do?" Basi asked.

"You're a hacker. Try to find Baaqir," I requested.

"I am a hacker, but I'm not a magician. It's not easy to trace someone who has disposed of their phone and SIM card," Basi replied.

"Are you sure you can't do anything? Please, Basi," I urged.

"You mentioned he got rid of his phone and SIM card," Basi reiterated.

"He did," I confirmed.

"Well, there's one possibility, but it's a long shot. In my WhatsApp group, I have some friends who are also hackers. I can ask them for assistance. However, I can't guarantee that we'll be able to locate him," Basi explained.

"Please, take that chance. Rahman will request Mr. Venky, a lawyer, to file a lawsuit in the meantime," I said.

"Who is Mr. Venky?" Ankhitha asked.

"He's one of my schoolmates," I replied.

"All your schoolmates seem to be lawyers, police officers, or in some other public service profession. Quite the coincidence," Greeshma remarked.

"That's true," I said with a chuckle.

"I still can't believe this woman killed her husband for money. How can a woman be capable of such a thing?" Ankhitha's mother wondered.

"It's due to her greed, aunty," I explained. As I spoke, I noticed my phone in my pocket heating up. I took it out and asked Basi, "Why does my phone keep heating up?"

"It could be a battery problem. You should show it to a phone retailer; they can replace the battery," Basi suggested.

"So, Doctor, what's the next step?" Ankhitha asked.

"We'll have to wait for the court hearing to be scheduled. In the meantime, our priority is to locate Baaqir," I replied.

"Basi, please act quickly," Ankhitha implored, her frustration evident.

"Dude, I need some time to work on this," Basi responded.

CHAPTER TWENTY-TWO

Entering the courtroom is an experience that makes everyone anxious and agitated. Today is the scheduled reopening of the Anwar murder case, and Ankhitha and I are there together for the first time. The courthouse is crowded, with many trials currently in progress. As we stand near the entrance to the courtroom, Mr. Venky, dressed in a black lawyer's suit, a white shirt, glasses, and neatly combed hair, approaches us.

"So, are you both prepared? Our hearing is next," Venky says.

"I'm so nervous right now," Ankhitha admits.

"Don't be nervous," I reassure her.

"In any case, we have a strong evidence. Don't worry; we have a video of Linsha's confession," Venky assures us.

"Hope so, buddy; it's all in your hands," I replied . As Linsha and her parents arrive, I notice them sitting on a bench outside the courtroom. After a while, a man in a lawyer's coat and a French beard approaches them. Venky is visibly shocked when he sees him.

"Adv Raghav Ramakrishnan?" Venky exclaims, "He's their attorney?"

"Do you know him?" I asked.

"He has never lost a case in court. He's too sharp," Venky says fearfully.

"Don't be pessimistic right now. While he may have won some legal battles, there's no guarantee he'll continue to do so," I reassure him.

"I need a juice right now; where can I get one?" Ankhitha asks.

"Over there," Venky points to the canteen, which is located next to the courtroom but a short distance away. Linsha and her father are seen heading towards the canteen.

"I'll get you a fruit drink," I told Ankhitha before heading to the canteen. I overheared Linsha and her father talking as I approach the canteen counter.

"You've compromised our family's reputation, Linsha. I regret having a daughter like you. You'll tarnish our family's name, and it will be because of you," Linsha's father, Raees, berated her. I see Linsha in tears as her father hurried towards the courtroom. When she catches my gaze on her, she wipes away her tears and enters the courtroom.

"10 rupees," the shopkeeper suddenly shouted. I walked back to where Ankhitha and Venky were waiting after getting the fruit drink. I can't help but feel a slight sense of unease and the feeling that I might be missing something. I've made my decision, so let's be truthful in court.

*****

In the dimly lit courtroom, the anticipation hung heavy in the air as Judge Roberts entered and took his seat at the bench. The rustling of papers and whispered conversations grew quiet as he cleared his throat and began to read the case of Anwar's untimely demise.

As the judge began reading the case file, a hushed murmur grasped the courtroom. This was no ordinary trial. The accusation against Linsha was the murder of her husband, Anwar, three years ago. Curiously, the case had been closed as an accident back then. The question everyone had was why it was now being reopened.

The judge peered over his spectacles and addressed the prosecutor, Venky, who stood confidently before the jury. "Mr. Venky," he began, "can you please explain to the court why this case has been brought back to our attention?"

Venky approached the podium, his voice composed but filled with conviction. "Your Honour, ladies and gentlemen of the jury, this case is not as it seemed three years ago. It is a tale of manipulation, deceit, and a woman's desperate quest for independence."

Gasps echoed throughout the courtroom, eyes widened with intrigue.

Venky continued, "This is a case of a woman's unwanted feministic attitude, wherein Linsha sought to become indebted and claim her husband's insurance money by murdering him. She planned meticulously, searching for the perfect opportunity to strike, all the while disguising her true intentions with a facade of love and devotion."

Whispers spread like wildfire amongst the spectators, a mixture of disbelief and shock flickering through the faces present.

"But," Venky's voice grew lower, his eyes never wavering from Linsha's icy stare, "Anwar's parents refused to accept the verdict that their beloved son's death was a mere accident. They were haunted by uncertainty and incessant doubts, pushing them to reopen the investigation."

"The evidence," Venky continued, "was concealed, manipulated, and staged by Linsha's own brother - Baaqir. A medical student who possessed the knowledge and skills to fabricate a car accident, creating the illusion of a tragic incident."

"The truth cannot remain obscured forever," Venky proclaimed with conviction. "Justice must prevail, for the sake of Anwar, his grieving parents, and the ideals this courtroom upholds."

As Venky moved back to his seat, the tension in the room intensified. Linsha's eyes darted from face to face, searching for support, for a shred of doubt in the eyes of the jury.

Adv Raghav stood up, exuding calm confidence, and adjusted his black robe. "Your Honour, esteemed members of the jury, ladies and gentlemen, Mr. Venky's claim is nothing but an inaccurate portrayal of the events that transpired. The truth is far more complex and revolves around the love and devotion Linsha had for her husband."

Raghav paced the floor, his eyes fixed on the jury as he began his defensive introduction. "Anwar's parents had long disapproved of his relationship with Linsha. They believed that his marriage to her was a ploy to obtain his fortune. As the facts will show, Linsha never benefited financially from her husband's death."

The defense attorney continued, marshaling his arguments with precision. "It is true that Linsha received an insurance payout after Anwar's accident. But that money was not a motive for murder."

Raghav turned toward Anwar's parents, his gaze stern. "Members of the jury, the prosecution's attempt to paint Linsha as a cold-hearted murderer is a calculated fabrication to get their hands on the insurance money. They seek to take advantage of her vulnerability by framing her for a crime she did not commit."

He paused for effect, allowing his words to sink in before continuing with conviction. "The truth will come to light, and we will hear from witnesses who can attest to Linsha's unyielding love for her husband. She would never harm a hair on his head, let alone take his life."

As Raghav took his seat, he glanced back at Linsha, offering her an encouraging smile. She clung to his words, hoping that justice would prevail.

Seeking permission from the judge, Venky requested to bring Anwar's parents in for questioning. The judge nodded in agreement, allowing the elderly couple to take the stand.

With a stern expression, Venky approached Anwar's father and questioned, "What made you believe that your son's wife, Linsha, could be responsible for his murder?"

Anwar's father took a deep breath before responding, his voice filled with anguish, "Linsha is a greedy woman. She loved money and her business more than my son. We knew she had taken numerous loans from banks and even borrowed from someone named Praman. The only way for her to repay these debts was to eliminate Anwar. We strongly believe that Linsha, along with her brother Baaqir, planned and murdered my son."

Venky listened attentively, mentally noting the information provided by Anwar's father. He saw an opportunity to solidify his case further and turned towards the judge. Confidently, he submitted a set of bank statements as evidence, showcasing the repayment of the loan after Anwar's death. He continued, "Your Honour, these are the bank statements that the defense's client, Linsha, submitted. They clearly indicate that she repaid a significant amount of money shortly after Anwar's demise. This raises suspicions about her motives."

Gasps could be heard throughout the courtroom as Venky's evidence painted a damning picture. To further emphasize his point, he produced another set of documents, stating, "Furthermore, this is the insurance claim that Linsha received after Anwar's death. It seems that financial gain was a significant motive behind her actions."

The judge glared at Linsha, taking a moment to absorb the presented evidence. The courtroom fell into a heavy silence as everyone awaited the judge's response. Linsha's face paled as she tried to come up with a response, her eyes darting nervously around the room.

"So, Mr. Zubair, you truly believe that Linsha, an innocent woman who lost her husband, killed him for his money? Are we to assume that all wives are guilty of murdering their husbands, merely for financial gain?" Adv. Raghav asked.

The question hung heavy in the air, followed by a deafening silence. The audience pondered the absurdity of such a notion, and a few muffled chuckles escaped their lips before erupting into laughter.

Adv. Venky, livid with anger, stood up once again, ready to interrupt the proceedings. But the judge warned, "Don't mock him; this is your warning, Adv. Raghav." Following his apology, Raghav resumed his cross-examination.

Adv. Raghav, fueled by the growing support in the room, pressed on. He reached for a folder containing the bank statements related to the insurance money settlement. With a grin of satisfaction, he laid out the evidence and presented it to Anwar's father.

"Let's take a look at these bank statements, shall we? You claimed that Linsha killed her husband for his money, to repay her loan. But here, in black and white, we can see that the insurance money was actually credited to a bank account. The very same account that Anwar opened under Linsha's name."

A wave of gasps rippled through the courtroom as the truth of Anwar's intentions began to unfold. Adv. Raghav's words reverberated in the minds of the audience, casting doubt upon the accusations.

Adv. Raghav continued, his voice filled with conviction, "You see, it's a common practice among Indian husbands. They manipulate their wives' bank accounts to evade taxes. Anwar opened this account for Linsha, but she never used it. Not a single transaction was made after his death."

The room fell silent once more, the weight of Adv. Raghav's words sinking in. But he wasn't finished.

"Now, let me ask you, Mr. Zubair, how did Linsha actually repay her loan? If she had no access to the insurance money, then where did the funds come from? It was Linsha's father who sold one of his lands to repay the debt, as shown in this selling agreement."

As Adv. Raghav's words echoed in the court, my mind raced to make sense of the puzzling scenario.

"In the investigation, we found the only motive why Linsha murdered Anwar was to get her husband's insurance money, isn't it?" Ankhitha asked me, her voice interlaced with skepticism.

Sighing deeply, I leaned back in my chair, contemplating the question. "Even though I got confused, if this wasn't the motive, what could be the real motive?" I mused, voicing my doubts aloud.

After hearing Adv Raghav's statement , the court questioned Adv. Venky, saying, "This case is over before it even began; if Linsha genuinely murdered her husband for the motivate you have presented, Adv. Raghav's words are discrediting your theory."

"I realise that seems to go against my idea," stated Adv. Venky as he stood to speak. "However, Linsha admitted to killing her spouse in a confessional video. According to Anwar's parents' complaint, police inspector Rahman put Linsha's confession statement into custody. To your owner, I would like to present the confession video."

As the courtroom settled into a hushed anticipation, Adv. Venky walked confidently towards the judge's bench, holding a pen drive in his hand. The air felt heavy with uncertainty, as everyone wondered what they were about to witness.

Adv. Raghav stared at Adv. Venky with a mix of disbelief and curiosity. He had been prepared to dismantle the defense's argument. The judge, with a raised eyebrow, motioned for Adv. Venky to proceed.

Adv. Venky connected the DVD player to a large monitor, taking a moment to compose himself before pressing play. The screen flickered to life, revealing a dimly lit room and an agitated Linsha sitting at a table. The sound of heavy breathing filled the courtroom, as the audience leaned forward, desperate to catch every word.

In the video, Linsha's tear-streaked face was a mask of desperation and despair. She began to speak, her words a chilling admission of her involvement in her husband's death.

"I can't take it anymore," Linsha said, her voice trembling. *"Anwar came to my flat unexpectedly that day. I begged him for money to help pay off my loans, but he couldn't provide the funds due to the COVID situation affecting his business. I was desperate and had to find a way to repay the money. As far as I could remember, Anwar had a life insurance policy. So, I had to get the money. I grabbed a rod from the main hall, hit him with it hard, and then again. When I checked his pulse, he had none. I called my brother Baaqir since I didn't know what to do. When he arrived, he took Anwar's body away and placed it in a large duffle bag. After that, I'm not sure what Baaqir did to cover it up, but he made it look like an accident in some way."*

Adv. Raghav watched the confession video intently, searching for any sign of manipulation or coercion. Linsha's words were raw and unfiltered, reflecting the anguish she had carried within her.

"As you have watched the confession video," Adv. Venky began, his voice filled with determination, "your honour, Linsha, confessed and also mentioned that her brother Baaqir covered it up."

The room murmured in disbelief as the shocking revelation sank in. Linsha, who had maintained her innocence throughout the trial, now appeared to be caught in a web of lies.

Adv. Venky continued, "Other than that, we have an eyewitness, Ms. Ankhitha, who saw the murder in the opposite flat on July 19, 2020, around 2:00 a.m. ."

Ankhitha entered the bustling courtroom, her nerves tingling with anticipation. The walls echoed with the hushed whispers of lawyers and onlookers, all anxiously awaiting the start of the trial. As she took her seat in the witness stand, she glanced towards the prosecution table, where Adv. Venky, sat waiting for her testimony.

Adv. Venky rose to his feet, a mix of curiosity and determination evident on his face. "Miss Ankhitha," he began, his voice firm yet comforting, "thank you for coming forward as an eyewitness to this heinous crime. Can you please tell us what you saw?"

Ankhitha took a deep breath, her mind drifting back to that fateful evening. "I was sitting by the window of my apartment," she started, her voice trembling slightly. "I could see right into the victim's flat, and I observed a woman striking a man with a rod."

Adv. Venky paced deliberately in front of the jury, every movement calculated to sway their opinion. "Miss Ankhitha, did you get a clear view of the assailant's face? Can you positively identify the person responsible for this murder?"

"Although I didn't see the assultant's face, I did witness a woman striking Anwar." Ankhitha confidently stated that.

"Miss Ankhitha, isn't it true that it was nighttime when this incident occurred?" Adv. Raghav asked, his voice dripping with skepticism.

Ankhitha nodded, her confidence waning. "Yes."

Adv. Raghav pressed on, skeptically. "And isn't it possible that your description of the assailant could match numerous individuals in the vicinity? How can you be sure it was Linsha?"

Adv. Venky, sensing her distress, interjected, his voice filled with conviction. "Be patient, please. Mr. Raghav, we have additional proof that Linsha did commit the crime. Ladies and gentlemen of the jury, I implore you to remember that her account of the events leading up to the murder is credible and consistent. Your Honour,"

Adv. Venky said, raising his voice. "I would like to call Mr. Ravi, a security guard from the government hospital morgue, to shed some light on the events surrounding this peculiar case."

The judge, intrigued by the request, gave his consent, allowing Mr. Ravi to take the stand. As he approached the witness box, the room fell silent, all eyes fixated on him.

"Mr. Ravi," Adv. Venky began, "can you tell us about the circumstances that led to your involvement with the deceased and the accused, Baaqir?"

Mr. Ravi gulped nervously as he recounted his actions. "Your Honour, I deeply regret my choices. It started when I received an offer from a man named Baaqir. He offered a large sum of money in exchange for a dead body."

Venky pressed further, demanding an explanation. "And what did you do, Mr. Ravi?"

"I hesitated at first," Mr. Ravi confessed, his voice heavy with guilt. "But the temptation became too strong. I betrayed my duty as a security guard and succumbed to the allure of money. I agreed to sell Baaqir a dead body."

Adv. Venky's words resonated with the jury and the onlookers. They understood that Ankhitha's and Mr Ravi's testimony, carried significant weight. It provided a crucial timeline of events that implicated the accused in the crime.

"Anwar passed away at night on July 19, 2020, however the postmortem report indicates that he passed away on July 20, 2020. How did it occur? I'll clarify.," Adv. Venky asserted confidently, "Baaqir is a medical student and he also knows the flaws and how to manipulate forensic evidence. Baaqir bought another dead body from a mortuary," Adv. Venky revealed, his voice unwavering, "he bribed the security guard, and he confessed. to fudge the time of death in an autopsy report. Baaqir staged that body as Anwar's, and he hid the real body somewhere else."

Whispers erupted throughout the courtroom as the revelation sent shockwaves through the crowd. Baaqir's meticulously planned scheme seemed too outlandish to be true, but Adv. Venky's convincing arguments left little room for doubt.

"Due to the severe harm to its face, the body's face cannot be identified, however according to Anwar's licence, his clothing and phone were recovered in that car." Adv. Venky concluded, his gaze fixed on the jury, "He knows that in most car accident cases, if the relatives identify the body, they won't check the DNA."

The jury deliberated for what felt like an eternity before finally reaching a verdict. Linsha's eyes widened with anticipation as she awaited her fate.

"Everyone, I understand this is a delicate matter, but if we want to uncover the truth, we must approach this scientifically," Venky began, his voice filled with assurance. "I believe that the man buried in the graveyard may not be Anwar. And the only way to prove my theory is to conduct an exhumation, thats all your honour."

The courtroom buzzed with anticipation as the judge, Adv. Raghav, and Adv. Venky took their respective positions. Baaqir, the missing piece of the puzzle, was nowhere to be found. His absence had sparked curiosity among everyone involved in the case.

The judge, with a stern expression, addressed Adv. Raghav, "Where is Baaqir? I summon him to this hearing. His presence is crucial for the proceedings."

Adv. Raghav, known for his quick thinking, stood up confidently. "Your Honour, Baaqir's absence is unfortunate but irrelevant."

Adv. Venky frowned at the statement. "Your Honour, Adv. Raghav's words are nothing more than a desperate attempt to divert attention from the truth. Baaqir holds crucial information that will shed light on the matter at hand. We must find him."

The judge listened attentively before responding. "Adv. Raghav, your remark about Baaqir's testimony being unreliable might not hold true. Mr. Venky's theory may sound like a movie story, but sometimes the truth is stranger than fiction. I am willing to explore all possibilities in search of the truth."

As the courtroom hushed, the judge continued, "Considering the circumstances, I feel it is necessary to carry out the exhumation of the deceased's body and conduct a DNA test. This will help establish the veracity of the allegations made by Adv. Venky. We cannot ignore any lead that comes our way."

The judge's decision struck a chord of both excitement and apprehension among those present. The order was passed, and the exhumation was scheduled.

CHAPTER TWENTY-THREE

Me, Ankhitha, Greeshma, and Basi were sitting in Ankhitha's cozy flat, talking about what transpired in court.

"Have you found Baaqir yet?" Ankhitha questioned angrily. "Once Baaqir is located, the case can be solved. You assured us that finding him would be simple."

To which Basi said, "It's not that easy to locate someone as brewing coffee."

"Like you actually know how to brew coffee?" sarcastically, Greeshma uttered

"Hey, Basi," I said, leaning closer. "Do you think you can hack into Baaqir's Instagram account and trace his location?"

Basi grinned mischievously, clearly excited by the challenge. "Leave it to me," he replied confidently, reaching for his laptop.

Ankhitha, immediately warned us, "With his cleverness, Adv. Raghav can easily manipulate the case. We need to be careful and aware of the potential consequences."

Greeshma, chimed in, "I agree with Ankhitha, but if we can help bring a criminal to justice, it might be worth the risk."

We all nodded in agreement, acknowledging the potential dangers and promising to be cautious every step of the way. Basi's fingers flew over the keyboard, working with incredible speed and precision. Within minutes, he managed to hack into Baaqir's Instagram account and started tracing his whereabouts.

As we anxiously waited for results, the room fell eerily silent. The only sounds that broke the stillness were the quiet clicks from Basi's keyboard. A few minutes later, a look of triumph crossed his face.

"I found him!" Basi exclaimed, his voice brimming with excitement.

We gathered around Basi, peering at his laptop screen. An exact location, only a few miles away from Ankhitha's flat, appeared on the screen.

Greeshma's eyes widened,"What should we do now?" she whispered, her voice quivering with nervousness.

"We must notify Rahman," I replied, my voice matching her apprehension.

I gave Inspector Rahman a call and gave him Baaqir's location. Taking a puzzled look, I hung up the phone.

"What happened, doctor? You don't feel excited about catching Baaqir," Ankhitha asked me.

"Something is missing, Ankhitha," I said, my voice laden with frustration. "I can feel it now. We've rushed to judgment, made assumptions without truly understanding the entire picture."

"What is missing?" Ankhitha asked, curiosity evident in her widened eyes.

"We were wrong about Linsha's motive for killing her husband, Anwar," I confessed, my mind racing with possibilities. "The real motive is something else. We are really missing something."

Ankhitha frowned, her brow furrowed in confusion. "But doctor, Linsha confessed to the crime herself. Whatever the motive is, Linsha did kill her husband, and that is the crime. We must give Anwar justice."

I nodded solemnly. "You're right, Ankhitha. Linsha's actions cannot go unpunished. But to truly bring her to justice and uncover the whole truth, we must unravel the intricate web that surrounds this case."

My phone rang loudly. Startled, I glanced at the screen to see Rahman's name flashing across it. Curiosity piqued, I hurriedly answered the call.

"Arnab, we got him," Rahman's voice boomed through the speaker, filled with a mix of triumph and relief. "We are taking him into custody. The next day is our hearing; the truth will be revealed;

Linsha and Baaqir will be behind bars soon."

CHAPTER TWENTY-FOUR

As the sun rose on the day of the hearing, I made my way to the courthouse. The atmosphere thrummed with anticipation and determination, as people from all walks of life gathered with a shared goal in mind: to bring Linsha and Baaqir to justice.

With the full confidence of a pre-assumed victory, Adv. Venky entered the courtroom, radiating an air of prestige and assurance. His reputation as a formidable advocate preceded him, and it seemed as though no case could ever be too challenging for him. Determination gleamed in his eyes as he prepared to face off against the renowned Adv. Raghav.

In another corner of the courtroom, Linsha and her worried parents anxiously waited. Their hopes hinged on the outcome of the trial. Seated just a row in front of them, were Ankhitha and I, curious observers of the unfolding drama.

As the judge entered the room and began the session, the courtroom settled into an expectant hush. The weight of the pending verdict hung in the air, casting a somber atmosphere. Adv. Raghav began his opening statement, weaving his words with eloquence and confidence, captivating the attention of everyone present.

The defence attorney for Linsha, Adv. Raghav, came up and stated, "Your honour, everyone has already concluded that Linsha is guilty after viewing the video of her confession up to this point. However, the justification for killing Anwar that Adv. Venky provided is already known to be false; the prosecution was unable to provide the true reason. The confession video has convinced everyone. Your honesty and integrity, however, are different. I'd like to invite Dr. Ashwarya, Linsha's psychiatrist, to the witness bench."

A long-haired woman in glasses approaches the witness bench. Ankhitha and I were both in disbelief when we saw her face.

"Is this the same girl that goes for morning walks in the park near your apartment block with Linsha?" I questioned Ankhitha

"She is, really; I had no idea she was a psychiatrist." Ankhitha uttered

As Dr. Ashwarya took the witness seat, the courtroom was filled with a palpable tension. Adv Raghav stood tall, his piercing gaze fixed on the psychiatrist.

"Dr. Ashwarya," Adv Raghav began, his voice steady but filled with purpose, "Please tell the court about your professional relationship with Linsha, the accused."

Dr. Ashwarya looked composed as she answered, "I have been treating Linsha for the past year for anxiety and depression. Our sessions have been focused on helping her cope with various aspects of her personal life."

Adv Raghav nodded and continued his line of questioning. "And can you recall any specific conversations or discussions you had with Linsha regarding her state of mind or any potential conflicts she might have been experiencing?"

Dr. Ashwarya nodded and began, "Certainly, Adv. Raghav. Delusions are firm beliefs held by individuals despite strong evidence to the contrary. In Linsha's case, she firmly believes that she killed her husband, Anwar, even though the evidence shows otherwise."

Raghav raised an eyebrow, his voice tinged with skepticism. "But Dr. Ashwarya, if the evidence contradicts Linsha's belief, how can it be classified as a delusion?"

"Delusions are often irrational and illogical," Dr. Ashwarya explained patiently. "Although the facts suggest that Anwar's death was accidental, Linsha's delusion alters her perception of reality. It amplifies her guilt and creates a false narrative that she is responsible for her husband's demise."

Adv. Raghav leaned back, his expression pensive. "Is it possible that Linsha's belief is rooted in a desire to take responsibility for Anwar's death, rather than being a delusion? Perhaps she feels an overwhelming amount of guilt for an accident and is creating this delusion to cope."

Dr. Ashwarya paused, considering Adv. Raghav's perspective. "While it is plausible that guilt could contribute to Linsha's mindset, the consistent presence of the delusion suggests a deeper psychological condition. Linsha genuinely believes she killed her husband, despite all the evidence pointing to the contrary."

Adv. Raghav pressed further, his voice assertive. "But is there any chance that Linsha's delusion is a result of manipulation? Could someone have influenced her to believe she killed her husband?"

Dr. Ashwarya shook her head, a touch of compassion in her eyes. "I have conducted extensive evaluations, gathering Linsha's medical history and interviewing her close associates. There is no evidence to suggest any external influence or manipulation at play. It's important to understand that delusions are subjective experiences, deeply ingrained in the individual's psyche."

Adv. Raghav's face revealed a mix of frustration and contemplation. After a brief pause, he cleared his throat and conceded, "Thank you, Dr. Ashwarya, for your insights into Linsha's delusional mindset."

As Dr. Ashwarya stepped down from the witness stand, the courtroom buzzed with the weight of her testimony. The judge and the members of the jury exchanged glances, grappling with the complexities of Linsha's case.

"According to the doctor Ashwarya's statement, it is evident that Linsha has been under a false belief that she killed her spouse Anwar," Adv. Raghav stated in court. "Thus, as Linsha's confessional video demonstrated, it is coincidental. Linsha has mental health issues and is naive. Furthermore, your honour, she didn't commit any crimes."

Prosecutor Adv. Venky took the stand and declared, "Let's just assume for a second that Linsha is a mental patient. What about Mis

Ankhitha, the witness who saw the murder? What about Baaqir, the brother of Linsha, who bought the body from the security guard? "Adv. Raghav, could you please explain?"

Clearing his throat, Adv. Raghav began, "Your honour, I understand the concerns raised by Adv. Venky, but we cannot solely rely on the accounts of the witnesses without thoroughly examining their credibility. Mis Ankhitha's statement, although seemingly convincing, could be influenced by external factors or mere misinterpretation. We need to dig deeper."

Turning to the jury, Adv. Raghav continued, "Now, let's focus on the security guard who allegedly sold the body to Baaqir. We must question the veracity of this claim. Is it possible that someone manipulated the situation in an attempt to frame Linsha for a crime she didn't commit?"

Adv. Venky scoffed, leaning against the prosecution table. "These are mere speculations, Adv. Raghav. We have concrete evidence that Baaqir bought the body. This proves her involvement in the crime. Your Honour," Venky said, looking directly at the judge. "I would like to bring Mr. Ravi to the witness bench."

Venky wasted no time. He pointed towards Baaqir, who was sitting quietly in the defendant's chair, and asked Ravi, "Is he the person who bought the body?"

After a brief pause, Ravi answered, "Yes, he is the one."

The room burst into whispers again. Adv. Raghav, stood up, clearly perplexed. "I am surprised, Your Honour," he said. "What does it make sense to show a random person and ask whether he bought the body or not?"

Venky remained calm. "Because this person is Baaqir, Linsha's brother," he said confidently.

Adv. Raghav raised an eyebrow and approached the person in question. "Are you really Linsha's brother?" he asked.

The person, who had been sitting silently, finally spoke. "No, sir," he said. "I am Munna. I live near the government hospital, and I work in a tea shop."

A moment of stunned silence enveloped the courtroom. The realization hit me like a wave of shock. The person we believed to be Baaqir, the key suspect of this crime, was, in fact, an innocent man named Munna.

Adv. Venky felt as though his entire world had been turned upside down. "Your Honour," he said, his voice filled with disbelief. "This means..."

Before he could finish his sentence, Munna pulled out his Aadhar card and voter ID card from his pocket and handed them to the judge. The evidence was undeniable. The cards proved that the person in question was indeed Munna and not Baaqir.

The courtroom erupted into chaos. Inspector Rahman, now in a state of confusion, tried to defend his initial accusation. However, it was clear that a grave mistake had been made.

As the dust settled, the judge called for order and addressed the court. "It seems we have made a grave error," he said solemnly. "Inspector Rahman, I expect an explanation for this unjust accusation."

Rahman stammered, trying to find words to justify his actions, but his profession pride had been shattered.

"On our first visit to Linsha's house, we spotted his picture. Is this the man we appeared to have seen in the photo?" Asking me, Ankhitha

"I even looked up Baaqir on Instagram and saw his picture. On Instagram, though, anyone can create a phoney ID." I stated

"Now, I'm completely perplexed. And just who is Baaqir? Is he somewhere?" Ankhitha asked

"I'm clueless. Our study is completely futile. All of the information we have discovered is false." I stated

"This is clear, Your Honour," Raghav exclaimed, his voice filled with conviction. "The evidence the prosecutor provided is essentially fabricated in an amateur way. They brought some random guy and said, 'This is Baaqir'; I mean, this is a disgrace to the court, Your Honour."

The judge, clearly perplexed by Raghav's outburst, raised an eyebrow and leaned forward. "I didn't understand anything here," he admitted, rubbing his temples. "But I do understand that Anwar died in a car accident."

"Your Honour, wait!" he interjected urgently. "We have one more crucial piece of evidence that is yet to be provided. The exhumation is done, and we haven't received the results yet. I am sure that the DNA result will be false, and that can prove our theory."

The judge, now even more intrigued, leaned back in his chair. The atmosphere in the courtroom was heavy with anticipation as the judge sternly addressed the room, "Where is the DNA report?" His words echoed, leaving a silence that seemed to hang in the air.

Several tense moments passed as the tension grew palpable. Then suddenly, a door at the back of the courtroom swung open, and a figure stepped forward, holding a sealed envelope.

Venky walked swiftly to the bench and said "Your Honour, inside this envelope is the analysis report of the DNA samples that were taken."

The judge took the envelope, his hands trembling ever so slightly. He carefully tore it open and pulled out the DNA report. With the eyes of everyone in the room fixed upon him, he unfolded it and started reading silently, his brows furrowing deeper with each passing moment.

Finally, the judge looked up, his gaze sharp and piercing. Addressing the crowd, he declared, "The DNA report shows that the body is indeed Anwar's."

Both Ankhitha and I were completely stunned at hearing this.

"How on earth is it even feasible? It completely upends our investigation." Ankhitha remarked

"At this moment, I am unable to comment. Though I felt something was missing, I didn't anticipate that everything we discovered was really a distraction." I spoke

The judge's stern voice boomed across the court, "After seeing the DNA report, it is convinced that the body buried in the graveyard is indeed Anwar's."

The courtroom erupted in gasps and whispers as the revelation sunk in. Linsha, who had maintained her innocence throughout the trial, stood visibly shaken but relieved. Meanwhile, Anwar's parents, who had waged war against her, looked stunned at the revelation. Their accusations had turned out to be false, and they now faced the consequences of their actions.

Judge continued, his voice unwavering. "All accuracies on Linsha have been vented off. Under Section 211 of the Indian Penal Code, which states that for the false allegation done on Linsha by Mr. and Mrs. Zubair, they have to be imprisoned in jail for 7 years and give compensation for 5 lakhs for Linsha."

It was an unexpected moment in my life. I still couldn't believe where I went wrong while investigating this case. I saw Linsha walking out of the court freely, even though Ankhitha and I knew that she had killed her husband. The evidence was there, but somehow the scenario had come back to where it started - unanswered.

Ankhitha and I had tirelessly worked on this case for months. We had followed every lead, unearthed countless secrets, and pieced together a thorough investigation. Yet, the more we delved into the lives of Linsha and Baaqir, the more confusing the truth became. the most anticipating question is that in the photo of Baaqir we saw on Instagram and the family photo of Linsha, the person shown in them wasn't Baaqir.

As we watched Linsha disappear into the crowd outside the courthouse, my mind raced with questions. Why did she kill her husband? How did Baaqir cover up the crime? And perhaps the most perplexing question of all: who was the real Baaqir?

3 Months later

CHAPTER TWENTY-FIVE

As I entered the cozy cafe, I couldn't help but feel a sense of anticipation mixed with apprehension. It had been a while since I had seen Ankhitha, Basi, and Greeshma, and now we were finally going to sit down and discuss the haunting mystery of Anwar's death.

The official report had ruled it as a simple accident, but my gut feeling told me otherwise. There were too many loose ends and unanswered questions for it to be a mere accident. I had spent countless nights pouring over evidence, and tirelessly following leads.

Now, as I approached their table, I noticed how the three of them had changed. Ankhitha, once known for her vibrant energy, seemed lost in her thoughts, her eyes filled with chaos. Basi, the funny and logical one, while Greeshma, the calm and composed friend, looked stoic but curious.

"Hey," I said, as a smile crept onto my face.

They rose from their seats simultaneously, a mix of surprise and warmth on their faces. Hugs were exchanged, and we settled down. The usual animated conversations and laughter were replaced by a heavy silence. Ankhitha broke the tension by voicing the thought that had been plaguing her mind for months.

"I still can't get over the fact that Linsha, the murderer, escaped so easily from the law," she said, her voice filled with disbelief.

Basi looked at Ankhitha, his dark eyes reflecting her frustration. "I agree, Ankhitha. It's hard to comprehend how someone so twisted can manipulate the system to their advantage."

Greeshma rested her hand on Ankhitha's shoulder, offering a reassuring touch. "The judicial process can be flawed at times, my dear friends. We must remember that justice doesn't always prevail, but that doesn't mean we should lose hope."

"But the evidence was clear, Greeshma!" Ankhitha exclaimed, frustration tinged with anger. "How could the court not see the truth that we all saw?"

Basi leaned forward, his voice filled with determination. "Sometimes, the truth can be clouded by manipulation and deceit. Baaqir was cunning enough to exploit the loopholes in the justice system, creating doubt where there should have been none."

Greeshma nodded, her wise eyes scanning the café, filled with empathy for her friends. "True justice might have evaded us this time, but let us not forget the power of unity. We must remain vigilant and work together to ensure such travesties do not go unanswered."

Ankhitha, feeling a surge of determination within her, wiped away a stray tear from her cheek. "You're right, both of you. We might not have been successful in court, but that doesn't mean we should allow Linsha to roam free. We must find another way to bring her to justice."

Greeshma arched an eyebrow, a hint of a smile playing on his lips. "And what do you suggest we do, Ankhitha? We cannot take the law into our own hands."

Ankhitha's eyes sparkled with determination as she leaned in closer. "No, but we can become investigative sleuths, gathering evidence and building a case against Linsha. We'll uncover the truth and expose her for the criminal she is."

Basi chuckled softly, her resilience shining through. "Well then, let's form our own justice league. An alliance against those who think they can evade the consequences of their actions."

They kept blathering on, and I lost it and interrupted. "I'm glad you guys agreed to meet," I began, my voice filled with determination. "I've been digging deep into Anwar's case, and I stumbled upon something that I believe could finally unlock the truth."

Ankhitha's hands clasped together, her nails tapping nervously against each other. Basi leaned forward, his analytical mind processing every word, and Greeshma remained serene, her eyes reflecting a calm determination.

"What is the reality? Did Linsha really kill her husband?" Ankhitha asked, her voice filled with uncertainty.

I took a deep breath before responding, "You saw the murder, Ankhitha. You can't deny what your own eyes witnessed."

Ankhitha's face grew troubled as she confided, "After the court sessions, I am unable to trust my own memory. Doubt has clouded my recollections, and I find myself questioning everything."

With a sympathetic smile, Greeshma chimed in, "It's not unusual for traumatic events to affect our memories. The mind can play tricks on us."

Feeling a rush of determination, I said, "Well, let me say it in chronological order. We were all investigated solely about Linsha. But we haven't given much thought to investigating the victim's personality. Since the motive for the murder we found out was wrong, I started researching the victim, Mr. Anwar."

Ankhitha's eyes widened with curiosity, urging me to continue.

"Remember Priya, Linsha's friend?" I asked. "I met her husband, Mr. Rajesh, who happens to be a close friend of Anwar. I met him a month ago, and he revealed some astonishing information about Anwar's character. I believe he provided the answer, too. "

"What is it, Arnab?" Ankhitha asked, her eyes filled with curiosity. I looked at her and smiled, unable to contain my excitement.

"Ankhitha, you won't believe what I found out about Anwar," I began, my voice brimming with anticipation.

CHAPTER TWENTY-SIX

1 month ago

I met Anwar's close friend, Rajesh, in a bustling mall. We had connected through social media and decided to meet in person to share stories about Anwar. As we sat down in a restaurant, Rajesh's troubled expression caught my attention.

"I am certain that Linsha killed Anwar because of whatever sort of relationship she had with him. I initially believed there to be an alternate explanation. it wasn't, though. The only person who knows more about Anwar, in my opinion, is you. I need your help man." I asked,

Rajesh hesitated for a moment before finally speaking. "There's something I need to tell you about Anwar," he said, his voice filled with both sadness and anger. He approached me with a solemn expression on his face. He seemed burdened by something he needed to share. "I have to tell you about Anwar's past," he confessed, a tinge of sadness in his voice. "It's something that has haunted me for years."

He began, "Anwar's character has always been a subject of curiosity for me. We were inseparable once, but after witnessing his actions in high school, I couldn't look at him the same way. It all stemmed from a single incident, an incident that still haunts me to this day."

Rajesh took a deep breath, collecting himself before continuing. "It was during our final year at school. Anwar's ego had grown to an unbearable extent, making him believe he was invincible. He was captain of the basketball team, which only fueled his ego even more."

"One afternoon, the school was buzzing with excitement as a group of new students joined the class. Among them was a timid, young boy named Rahul, who wore a constant look of fear on his innocent face. Little did Rahul know that his path would soon cross with Anwar's, forever changing both their lives."

"Anwar saw Rahul as an easy target to assert his dominance," Rajesh lamented. "He would mock and tease Rahul relentlessly, belittling him every chance he got. His bullying was subtle, yet potent enough to break Rahul's spirit."

As days turned into weeks, the bullying escalated. Anwar would discreetly torment Rahul in the school corridors, behind the backs of teachers and oblivious to the pain he was causing.

Rajesh's voice wavered as he recounted the darkest moment. "One day, my eyes caught sight of something I never thought I would witness. Anwar dragged Rahul into an empty classroom, his ego surpassing all limits. The sounds of muffled cries and fear emanated from behind the closed door."

When I learned this, I was stunned. I was curious: "Did he suffer any repercussions as a result of that?"

"You already know that his parents are incredibly wealthy. And no matter what he does, his parents don't stop him; instead, they hide and support him. As a result, if someone hurts his ego, he won't stop until they are totally destroyed." Rajesh remarked, his eyes filled with terror.

I inquired with curiosity, "I heard through your wife, Priya, that Linsha and Anwar's connection went beyond love."

"Priya is still oblivious to Anwar's true face. Anwar's parents are proficient in it. They are skilled manipulators who can make others do what they want while still coming across as kind and joyful. Anwar is occasionally hazardous on the inside, though. If someone ignores him, he cannot stand it. Sometimes he acts in an irrational manner." Rajesh said

Curiosity piqued, I leaned forward, encouraging him to continue. Rajesh took a deep breath and began recounting an incident that had left a deep scar on him.

"Anwar used to molest his wife," Rajesh whispered, his words hanging heavy in the air. "It all started when they disagreed on certain matters, and she didn't always obey him. He thought he had the right to control her and used his power to exploit her physically."

Rajesh continued, "Years ago, when I returned home unexpectedly and found Anwar standing over Linsha, his hands trembling with anger. It was a horrifying sight I will never forget. His wife lay there, bruised and broken, the light in her eyes snuffed out. I learned that she was pregnant and had chosen to terminate the pregnancy a few weeks later. I firmly believe that her decision to have an abortion was a direct result of the molestation she endured."

Shock washed over me as I tried to process what Rajesh had just shared. This was not the Anwar I knew - the friendly, charismatic guy who always seemed respectful and caring. It was difficult to reconcile these two contrasting images.

Rajesh continued, his eyes filled with pain. "At first, she kept this torment hidden, fearing the shame it would bring to their families. But one day, she could no longer bear it and confided in me. Hearing her heart-wrenching account shattered my trust in Anwar. I couldn't fathom how someone we considered a dear friend could engage in such despicable acts."

Linsha had suffered silently, enduring the torment of abuse behind closed doors. It was a never-ending cycle of power, control, and manipulation that had left her emotionally scarred. Rajesh shared the immense guilt he felt for not noticing the signs sooner, blaming himself for not protecting her from such abuse.

Rajesh added, "When I learned that Anwar was abusing his wife Linsha, I asked about it to Anwar"

RAJESH SPEAKS

"How dare you?" Anwar hissed through clenched teeth. "Your curiosity will be the death of you, Rajesh. If you ever utter a word about what you think you know, I will personally ensure that you suffer the consequences."

I confronted the fear that was constricting his heart, my voice quivering as I mustered the courage to ask, "Why? Why would you inflict such pain upon your wife?"

Anwar's gaze hardened as he released his grip on me, taking a step back but keeping an intimidating presence. "You know nothing of the masks we wear, Rajesh. Linsha and I hold secrets that were never meant to be exposed. It is not yours to understand nor interfere."

Though silenced by Anwar's threats, I couldn't simply ignore the truth he had stumbled upon. But the fear of confronting the monster hidden behind the neighbourly façade paralysed him. Days turned into weeks, yet the secret continued to weigh heavily on his conscience.

During this time, I couldn't help but observe Linsha's gradual deterioration. The vibrancy that once defined her had faded, replaced by a hidden sadness that dwelled within her eyes. The pain she carried seemed to scream out for help, begging for release from the torment that chained her.

It was a peaceful evening, the warm rays of the setting sun casting a golden hue upon the quiet suburban neighbourhood. I had just arrived home after a long day at work, longing for nothing more than to relax and forget about the stress of the day. Little did I know that tranquility was about to give way to chaos and danger.

As I stepped inside my house, I noticed a figure lurking in the shadows of the hallway. My heart skipped a beat as recognition washed over me. It was Anwar, who had always seemed a bit off, but I never suspected him of harbouring a dark secret.

Anwar's eyes were filled with a mix of desperation and fear. His trembling hands clutched something tightly behind his back. Before

I could react, he lunged toward me, his attacks fierce and brutal. Shocked and bewildered, I could barely defend myself against his vicious onslaught.

My mind raced, trying to make sense of what was happening. Why was Anwar attacking me?

Finally, I managed to dodge his blows and gain some distance between us. Blood trickled from cuts and bruises that adorned my face and body. Fear and determination coursed through my veins as I locked eyes with Anwar, his face contorted with rage.

"You don't understand!" he spat, his voice laden with desperation. "I have to protect the secret! I can't let anyone find out!"

Confusion and anger mingled within me, but a stubborn resolve pushed me to my feet. "Tell me, Anwar," I demanded, my voice wavering but firm. "Tell me what this secret is worth. Is it worth hurting innocent people, worth destroying lives?"

With a sudden surge of strength, I lunged forward, catching Anwar off guard. We wrestled, grappling with each other as the struggle unfolded with frenzied intensity. Adrenaline fueled my movements, allowing me to hold my own against his unexpected brutality.

ARNAB'S NARRATION

"I am afraid of Anwar, because of that incident. Not even my wife knew about it." Rajesh spoke in a terrified tone.

After learning all of this, I discovered the explanation for Linsha's husband's death and the reason behind the mishandling of our investigation.

CHAPTER TWENTY-SEVEN

Present day

As I finished narrating the unsettling story of Anwar's abusive behaviour towards his wife Linsha, there was a heavy silence that hung in the air. Ankhitha, Greeshma, and Basi stared at me in shock, their eyes wide with disbelief.

"I can't believe this," she whispered, her hands trembling. "How could Anwar do this to her?" Ankhitha asked

I nodded solemnly. "Yes, Anwar suffered from narcissistic personality disorder. It's a mental health condition where individuals have an inflated sense of their own importance and a deep need for validation and admiration. These patients struggle to control their anger and often lack empathy for others."

Ankhitha asked "But how does someone develop such a disorder?"

"While the exact cause of narcissistic personality disorder is not known, some researchers believe that a combination of genetic, environmental, and social factors come into play," I explained. "In some cases, overprotective or neglectful parenting can impact children who are already predisposed to developing the disorder. Anwar's parents always indulged him and encouraged his every action. Even when he exhibited selfish and manipulative behaviour, it was always justified or overlooked."

"So this is the actual reason Linsha killed her husband," she said. "Not the utter nonsense we discovered about her." Ankhita stated

“According to Rajesh, Anwar’s parents are highly skilled at concealing these facts since they place a higher importance on their reputation than Linsha’s misery. Additionally, Linsha’s parents valued their reputation over her life as well. The majority of Indian parents continue to do that.” I said

Ankhitha turned to me, her eyes filled with a mix of anger and confusion. "But how come our investigation went wrong?" she asked.

I leaned back in my chair, contemplating her question. "See, like it or not, people in our society still think that if a woman goes for a job, they become judgmental," I replied. "That is what happened here. While we were researching Linsha’s personality and background, people started saying bad things about her because they couldn’t see a girl starting a business.”

Ankhitha’s expression softened as the pieces started to fall into place. "Isn’t it the case that when we frequently encounter a lie, we tend to start accepting it as truth?" she asked, her voice tinged with both frustration and understanding.

I nodded. "Exactly. It’s when more people tell us about someone’s flaws or limitations, unknowingly, we start to believe them. The illusory truth effect, also known as the truth effect, is a cognitive bias that causes people to believe information is true after hearing it repeated frequently, even if it’s actually false. Despite her hard work and determination, rumours had spread like wildfire, tarnishing her reputation. People who had never met her began to form opinions based solely on hearsay and prejudice.”

“But there is one thing I still don’t understand: who is Baaqir? What exactly is his role here?” Greeshma questioned

“I found Baaqir, I know who he is.” I said

“Who is he?” Ankhitha enquired in wonder. "Tell me,"

"Little did I know, the truth was right in front of me.” With a slow, deliberate gesture, I pointed towards Basi and uttered those words that would unravel everything: ‘Here he is.’ As the tension hung in the air, I revealed the shocking twist, my voice barely above a whisper, “Basi is Baaqir.”

"What? How is it possible?" Greeshma exclaimed, her voice echoing through the cafe. "His name is Basi, not Baaqir, and we do know him."

Basi's eyes widened as all eyes turned to him. His face flushed with a mix of embarrassment and fear. Ankhitha and Greeshma exchanged confused glances, unsure of what to believe. Basi finally let out a nervous laugh, attempting to brush off the accusation.

"You must be mistaken," Basi stammered, his voice shaking. "My name is Basi, not Baaqir. I don't know where you got this idea from."

"Hmm, interesting," I replied, narrowing my eyes. "Because I happened to stumble upon some interesting information that suggests otherwise. You see, Baaqir is not just any name, it holds a significant meaning. It means 'he who knows' in Arabic. And trust me when I say, Basi here knows more than he's letting on."

Basi's face paled, and his once confident demeanor crumbled. He knew he couldn't hide the truth any longer. He took a deep breath, visibly gathering his thoughts before speaking.

"This still defies belief. How come Basi........." Ankhitha uttered.

"Basi is his nickname; his real name is Baaqir, Ankhitha. Linsha's brother." I said

"How long have you been close friends with Basi?" I queried, turning to Ankhitha.

"3 years back. The first time I met him was when I invited him to my birthday party, as I recall. He is my neighbour even though he lives with his parents." Ankhita said

"He doesn't stay with his parents; he stays as a paying guest." I said. Greeshma and Ankhitha gave Basi a startled look.

"Basi, aka Baaqir, is one of the smartest guy I have ever seen," I began my explanation. "As I already stated, when Linsha opened her own company, everyone began spreading untrue rumours about her. That was a tactic Baaqir employed to hide Linsha's crime. Let me now explain how he managed to manipulate everything. As you mentioned, Ankhitha - Basi was away for two days during the murder occurrence that took place that day. That day, Linsha didn't know what to do at the time, so she called Baaqir. As soon as he arrived, he removed Anwar's body from the crime scene and placed it in a huge duffel bag on wheels.

He took Anwar's body and kept it in Anwar's car, then drove to the Palakkad Komaram Hotel and checked in under Anwar's name by showing the front desk employee his Adhaar card. I'm still puzzled by how he manipulated the time of death in autopsy report, though. Whatever it was, when he got back to the flat after two days, he learned about you, Ankhitha, that you had witnessed the murder and the reason why those around you weren't buying the account. Basi kept hanging around with you so he could anticipate your next move. He knew that someday someone would take your story seriously. That's why he began assembling fictitious witnesses and evidence earlier. As a result of his visit to Pallakad Mortuary, he learned that the security had previously been selling the corpses. Afterward, Munna, an adolescent resident of the slums, came into view. To manipulate the scenario and arrest the wrong person, Basi offered him money, had him pose for photos while wearing his clothes, made up the name Baaqir on a fake Instagram account, and used Photoshop to substitute Munna's picture for Linsha's family photo. In order to provide a fake witness, Munna was asked by Basi to buy a dead body from security. However, he only purchased the deceased body in order to fabricate a tale of body swapping and deflect our investigation. but, he didn't actually use that body for anything. He might have interred elsewhere. He waited after that. And after three years, I finally showed up and started helping you, Ankhitha. I asked Basi to hack Linsha's Instagram, but he hacked my phone instead. That is the cause of the sporadic heating up of my phone. He expertly manumitted us because he was aware of all our nuances. Additionally, he gave me access to the Linsha and Baaqir false bot accounts, which caused the investigation to be misdirected by displaying fake chat exchanges."

The weight of the secret had lifted off my shoulders, but as I looked at their shocked faces, uncertainty flooded my heart.

Basi had always been the center of their close-knit group of friends. His charismatic personality and easy charm attracted us like moths to a flame. We had spent countless evenings laughing and sharing stories, unaware that a web of lies was coiling around us.

Ankhitha, with her gentle nature and warm smile, was the first to regain her composure. She looked at me with a mixture of confusion and hurt, searching for answers. Greeshma, always the pragmatic one, silently appraised the situation, her analytical mind processing the truth.

"You mean to tell me that everything we know about Basi is a lie?" Ankhitha asked, her voice trembling with disbelief.

I nodded solemnly. "Yes, I'm afraid so. Basi has been fabricating stories and manipulating us all this time."

“How did you discover the truth, though?” Greeshma enquired.

“My sister spittled out his genuine name, Baaqir, as we were chatting about Basi.” and I turned to face Basi. “Now I see why you broke up with my sister, I guess that explains it. You decided that it would be preferable to end your relationship with her because I might end up hurting my sister in this situation, as a result of my involvement with Ankhitha's issue. I later ran across Munna, who claimed that Basi had given him some money and told him to follow his instructions.”

"But how is that even possible?" Ankhitha remarked, her tone tinged with disbelief. "We didn't even notice his presence when Linsha was with her parents, and there was seemingly no connection between them."

I chimed in, shedding some light on the situation. "It's because he had distanced himself from his parents for several years due to a significant disagreement. This dispute arose from how he and my sister interacted with them and an underlying intercaste issue. He cleverly used this estrangement as a cover to conceal his sister's involvement in the crime."

After a brief pause, Ankhitha's curiosity got the better of her, and she couldn't help but ask, ‘But why did Linsha suddenly decide to confess at the police station?’ Her question hung in the air, demanding an answer that could unravel the mystery behind

Linsha's unexpected confession.

"Basi was aware that Linsha was unable to maintain her confidentiality. She can blow everything up with just a single spark. To establish an alibi that she was delusional, Basi asked one of his friends, Dr. Ashwarya, to accompany her. Her confession wasn't entirely accurate, either. The motive wasn't right." I said

After learning all of this, Greeshma and Ankhitha were startled. I saw the conflicting emotions flickering in Basi's eyes. There was guilt, remorse, but also a glimmer of hope. He had expected condemnation, judgment, and the end of his freedom. But instead, I was offering him a chance to turn his life around, to use his skills for a greater purpose.

"The police aren't here, so don't worry. not intending to imprison you." I chuckled as I said it.

"What are you going to do then?" Ankhitha hesitated before asking.

"Imagine a world where every woman can feel safe, where they don't have to live in fear," I continued, my voice filled with conviction. "With your intelligence and intuition, you can uncover the true nature of individuals, expose potential predators before they can cause harm. I understand why you covered up your sister's crime. Actually, your instance provided me with the solution I was seeking. the key to stopping a crime before it starts. Nothing will change if I allow myself to arrest you and lock you up. The same atrocities will occur again. Most Indian ladies experience the same problem that your sister Linsha had, in addition to just your sister. I have never seen a guy as smart as you. Basi, if you can cover up this crime ingeniously, you'll be able to learn a lot about someone else's personality. I want you to establish an agency. People only learn a small amount of information about the bride or groom in an arranged marriage. Before setting up a marriage, this agency is required to conduct a thorough investigation on that person's personality. By doing this, it is possible to prevent the molestation of millions of women. Will you do it? Basi?" I asked

Basi remained silent for a moment, deep in thought. The weight of his sister's experience and the countless other victims weighed heavily on his conscience. A new purpose had presented itself, an opportunity to make amends, not just for his sister but for all those suffering silently. Basi eventually got to his feet and turned around without saying anything. As Basi briskly made his way towards the exit, I felt a sense of urgency overpowering me. I couldn't let him leave without getting the answers I desperately sought. With determination burning in my eyes, I reached out, gently gripping his arm to stop him in his tracks.

"How did you change the time of death in the autopsy report? How did you do it?" I questioned, my voice trembling with curiosity and unease.

But as I had expected, he remained silent. After that, he left the café. This might be the only question that crosses my thoughts and the one notion that remains unresolved.

CHAPTER TWENTY-EIGHT

3 weeks later

Ankhitha came to my house one sunny afternoon, clad in her usual cheery demeanor. She handed me a small envelope with a mischievous glint in her eyes. "This is for you," she said, her voice filled with anticipation.

With trembling hands, I carefully slid the envelope open, unfolding the letter inside. Basi's words leapt off the page, written in his characteristic flowing script. As I began to read, his voice echoed in my mind.

'Dear Arnab,

I hope this letter finds you well. I wanted to let you know that I have taken up the offer you asked of me. I have decided to do the thing. There is also something else I need to tell you. Ankhitha told me about your first love—the woman you only chatted with over Facebook and have never met in person. She asked me to trace her, and you told her that her account username was Rockin Lin.

I found out about her, Arnab. She was my sister, Linsha - Lin for Linsha. I couldn't believe it at first, the coincidence of it all. Linsha, my dear sister who was taken away from us so many years ago. I couldn't help but wonder how different things could have been if life had taken a different turn.

You see, on that day you were supposed to meet at Al Wahda Mall, Linsha was just fifteen years old. It was a time of innocence and dreams, where the possibilities seemed endless. I remember her excitement as she prepared for the meeting. But fate had other plans for her. Our mother, driven by irrational fear and misguided intentions, intervened.

She saw Linsha's growing attachment to you and couldn't bear the thought of her being distracted from her studies and the goals she had set for her. Our mother took drastic measures to ensure her focus remained solely on academic pursuits, taking away her phone and dismantling it.

I know it sounds unbelievable, but it's true. Linsha was torn away from the chance to be with you, to live a life filled with happiness and love. It pains me to think about what could have been. Maybe fate intervened, or perhaps our parents made the wrong choice. Either way, it is a difficult truth to accept.

But Arnab, life goes on. We cannot dwell on the past or the what-ifs. Linsha's choices were taken away from her that day, but you still have a long life ahead of you. Find happiness, chase your dreams, and build a future filled with love.

Sometimes, in the grand tapestry of life, we encounter obstacles and missed opportunities. We may never understand why certain things happen or why paths diverge. But we must keep moving forward, living each day to the fullest, and cherishing the people and moments that bring us joy.

Take care, my friend, and know that I am here for you if you ever need someone to talk to."

"My god Linsha was Rockin Lin, Arnab, your first love." Ankhitha stated

"Yes, she is; I hadn't expected that," I said

"Sometimes, life can be cruel and unpredictable. It's unfortunate that Linsha had to go through such a painful experience with her husband."

I nodded, my face filled with sorrow as I remembered the once vibrant Linsha he had fallen in love with.

"But now, it seems punishing her wouldn't right the wrongs," Ankhitha continued. "Linsha has already endured unimaginable pain. Instead, what she needs is support and love."

"I wish things were different," Arnab whispered, fighting back tears. "I wish I had understood the depth of her suffering before."

Ankhitha touched my arm gently, offering comfort. "We can't change the past, Arnab. But we can learn from it. Linsha's strength is an inspiration to us all. Let it remind us to be more understanding and compassionate towards others."

"True" I replied.

"I still couldn't understand how Basi managed to change the time of death in the autopsy report for Anwar," Ankhitha asked, frustration bubbling within her.

"That is the only thing I couldn't find out." i said "Basi is known for being meticulous, calculating. If he indeed manipulated the time on the report, he would have had to employ an elaborate plan to do it without raising any suspicion."

"That's what bewilders me," Ankhitha admitted, running her fingers through her hair in exasperation. "Anwar's death wasn't accidental; it was a cold-blooded murder."

Ankhitha leaned back in her chair, analyzing the case from different angles. "Let's consider multiple possibilities," she suggested. "Was the autopsy report transmitted electronically?"

I furrowed my brows, racking my brain for the details. "Yes, it was sent digitally to the police station. The only physical copies were in the hands of the forensic team."

Ankhitha's eyes lit up, excitement evident in her voice. "Then perhaps the manipulation occurred during the transmission," she pondered. "Basi, being tech-savvy, could have hacked into the system and altered the details."

I nodded, intrigued by the possibility. "But how did he gain access to the internal police network without leaving any traces?"

Ankhitha pondered for a moment. "Basi is known for his exceptional computer skills," she said. "He might have hacked into the police station's network or manipulated the encryption protocol. It would require technical expertise, but it's not entirely implausible."

"But even if he tampered with the digital transmission, wouldn't someone notice the discrepancy later?" I asked, playing devil's advocate.

Ankhitha smiled, her eyes gleaming with determination. "Unless, he also manipulated the physical copies held by the forensic team," she said. "If he modified the time of death on the digital report and matched it with the physical copies, it would be difficult to detect his deception."

"These are merely theories, Ankhitha, although they might be true. I still have no idea how he did it. But what is the point after knowing it?" I asked

"Yes, there is no point. Basi is a shady character who will easily manipulate everything, even if we discover something. He managed to trick us for three years even using his nick name, Basi. His real name is Baaqir, which we only recently discovered." Ankhitha said with a smile.

Inside the envelop, I found a single card, embellished with elegant calligraphy and adorned with a golden wax seal.

It was a business card, pristine and professional in appearance, showcasing a sleek logo displaying the words "Baaqir Private Agency."

"So, as you requested, he did establish an agency." Ankhita stated

"Yes, he did; let's see if it can prevent the savagery towards woman that characterises the majority of arranged marriages." I said

At that point, my mother arrived and brought us coffee. Then, when she turned to face Ankhitha, she was about to ask a foolish question. She received a "get away" look from me. She looked at me angrily before returning to the kitchen. She wanted me to propose to her, and I was about to. but instead I asked something else.

"So, what's been keeping you so preoccupied lately?" I asked, taking a sip of my coffee.

Ankhitha's eyes sparkled with anticipation as she leaned forward, her voice barely containing her excitement. "I've decided to enroll in a culinary course!"

Ankhitha had always been fond of cooking, and I had witnessed her passion for experimenting with flavors and creating delicious meals.

"That's amazing, Ankhitha!" I exclaimed, a smile spreading across my face. "What made you decide to take this step?"

Ankhitha chuckled nervously, her fingers playing with the handle of her coffee cup. "Well, you know how much I love cooking, right? It's more than just a hobby for me. I've always felt this deep connection with food. It's a way for me to express myself, to bring joy to others through my creations."

As she spoke, her face radiated passion and determination. I could tell this was not a decision she made on a whim. Ankhitha had spent countless hours perfecting her skills in the kitchen, honing her techniques, and experimenting with various ingredients. Her love for culinary arts was undeniable.

"I want to learn more, explore different cuisines, and become a skilled chef," Ankhitha continued with a smile. "This culinary course will not only give me the necessary knowledge and techniques but also unlock doors to endless possibilities and opportunities."

Her words resonated with me, and a wave of excitement began to wash over me. I could envision Ankhitha as a prominent chef in a renowned restaurant, serving her unique creations to patrons from all over the world. Her passion and dedication were infectious, and I started to feel a surge of admiration for her decision.

"I'm really proud of you, Ankhitha," I said sincerely, reaching across the table to squeeze her hand. "You've always had this magic touch when it comes to cooking. I have no doubt that you'll excel in this culinary course and achieve great things."

A blush crept up Ankhitha's cheeks as gratitude filled her eyes. "Thank you so much for your support. It means the world to me."

Our conversation continued well into the evening, as we discussed Ankhitha's plans and aspirations. It was clear that she had thought this through meticulously, envisioning a future filled with culinary success. Listening to her talk about new flavors, innovative techniques, and the joy of creating gastronomic masterpieces left me inspired and craving for more.

As the sun began to set, we hugged each other tightly, embracing the excitement and anticipation that lay ahead. Ankhitha was embarking on a new journey, one that would empower her and allow her to share her culinary passion with the world. Although it didn't feel good to say goodbye, I could tell by the look in her eyes that she was more focused on advancing her culinary career than on finding a spouse. So I made the choice to back off. That is the best thing I can do for her because it follows a straightforward principle that everyone should understand: if you really like someone, let them go.

The Reality

(Revealing only from the viewpoint of the readers.)

July 19, 2020

CHAPTER TWENTY-NINE

Baaqir, better known as Basi, was feeling excited as he prepared himself to attend Ankhitha's birthday party. Ankhitha, a friend of Basi, had invited him two days ago, and he couldn't wait to celebrate with her.

Basi's sister, Linsha, had chosen to spend the night alone at her flat. She enjoyed the solitude, finding solace in the quiet evenings. But that night, everything changed when her husband, Anwar, unexpectedly appeared at her doorstep.

Anwar was furious that Linsha had stayed in her flat without informing him. He unleashed his uncontrolled anger, his voice filling the confined space with venomous words.

"Where have you been?" he demanded, his voice tinged with accusation. "I've been trying to reach you all day! Why didn't you answer my calls?"

Linsha's brows furrowed, her eyes widening in confusion. "Anwar, I'm so sorry," she began, her voice tainted with self-doubt. "I left my phone at work by mistake, and I didn't realize until just now."

Anwar's frustration turned into anger. "You left your phone? Just like that? Without caring about how worried I'd be? How could you be so thoughtless?"

When Linsha became frightened, she bolted the door to the bedroom. In a fit of rage, Anwar banged his fist against the door, causing the thin wood to splinter slightly. "Linsha!" he bellowed, his voice laced with venom. "Open up! We need to talk!"

His words echoed through the hallway, but there was no response from within. Anwar's anger intensified, and he slammed his fists against the door again and again. "How dare you ignore me! How dare you stay here without telling me!"

Finally, the door creaked open, revealing a disheveled Linsha, her eyes red and puffy from crying. She wordlessly gestured for Anwar to come in, her silence only fueling his anger further. He stormed inside, the confined space unable to contain his boiling emotions.

"What is wrong with you, Linsha?" Anwar spat, his words sharp enough to cut through the tense air. "How could you just disappear like that, leaving me worried sick? Do you have any idea what I've been going through?"

Linsha trembled, tears streaming down her face as she attempted to find her voice.

His rage soon turned into something far more sinister. Without warning, he crossed the line and began to molest her, ignoring her desperate pleas for him to stop. She attempted to flee by running towards the hall, but Anwar caught her.

Fear and adrenaline coursed through Linsha's veins as she realized she was left with no choice. In a desperate act of self-defense, she reached for the only thing within her grasp, a metal rod lying against the wall. With a trembling hand, she swung the rod towards Anwar, the force behind her strike fueled by a mixture of fear, anger, and a longing for freedom.

The rod connected with Anwar's head, and the sound that echoed through the room was sickeningly hollow. Anwar collapsed onto the floor, his eyes fluttering shut, forever silenced by the fatal blow.

His pulse could not be detected when Linsha examined it. She then realised Anwar was no longer alive. Her heart pounded in her chest as she stared at the lifeless body before her, her mind a whirlwind of emotions. She felt a strange mixture of relief, guilt, and grief. What had just happened? How had her reality spiraled into this grim situation?

Realizing she needed help, Linsha called Basi as her trembling voice struggled to explain what had occurred. Basi's initial excitement quickly turned to shock and concern as he listened to his sister recount the horrifying events of that night. Although he was frightened and uncertain, he resolved to be there for Linsha, providing whatever support she needed.

Basi rushed to Linsha's flat, his footsteps echoing the fear pounding in his heart .When he stumbled upon the shocking scene of his elder sister, Linsha, standing over a lifeless body, he knew he had to act swiftly. The sight of Anwar, Linsha's abusive husband, lying motionless on the floor, sent chills down his spine.

"What happened, Linsha?" he whispered, trying to keep his voice steady. "Why did you...?"

"He was going to kill me, Basi," she choked out, her voice trembling. "I had no choice. I couldn't let him hurt me anymore."

With a heavy heart, Basi rushed to his sister's side, embracing her tightly. Her eyes were filled with fear and desperation, her body trembling with the weight of what had just transpired. Basi consoled her, whispering reassuring words in her ear. "I'm here, Linsha. Don't worry, I will protect you. We will get through this together."

Realizing that they needed to act fast, Basi formulated a plan. Basi knew that the first step was to cover up the evidence and ensure the body would never be found.

With meticulous care, Basi retrieved a huge wheeled duffel bag that was tucked away in his garage. Gently, he lifted Anwar's lifeless body and placed it inside, zipping up the bag. Basi's hands shook as he secured the lock, knowing that the next actions he took would shape their destinies.

He made his way to the Anwar's vehicle, the duffel bag precariously hidden in the dicky tray. Basi knew that the security guard at the main entrance logged every vehicle that left the premises, but he saw an opportunity. The guard was presently occupied with handling a commotion in Block B with Ankhitha, leaving the entrance momentarily unattended.

Seizing the moment, Basi quickly slipped the vehicle past the gate, relieved that the guard's attention was elsewhere. The absence of his license plate in the log book would buy them precious time.

Driving away from the flat, a mixture of guilt and determination filled Basi's heart. He knew that what he had done was not ideal, but it was the best choice for his sister's safety. He carried the weight of their secret, the heavy burden of protecting the only family he had left.

He kept on driving. He arrived in Palakkad by car and spotted a motel. He reasoned that it might give him an alibi. an alibi to show that Anwar stayed here.

As Basi arrived at Komaram hotel, he concealed his identity wearing a carefully crafted mask. His face hidden, he approached the reception desk, determined to back up Anwar's alibi. "I'd like to check in under the name Anwar," Basi said, his voice stifled beneath the mask.

The hotel clerk nodded and scanned the Aadhar card Basi had handed over. "Everything seems to be in order, Mr. Anwar." Oblivious to the fact that he was dealing with someone other than Anwar, the clerk handed over the room keys, noting down the details for their records.

July 20, 2020

CHAPTER THIRTY

The next day in the evening, as the orange sun began to set, Basi's troubled mind propelled him on a fateful journey. Filled with a mix of desperation and determination, he made his way towards the secluded Attapadi Reserve Forest.

Driven by a desperate need to protect Linsha from further harm, Basi devised a plan. He would stage a car accident, making it appear as if Anwar had met a tragic end. It was a radical idea, one that twisted his insides with unease, but Basi saw no other way to guarantee his sister's safety.

When he arrived at the chosen spot, anxiety knotted in Basi's stomach. He had carefully planned how to make it look like an accident, but he couldn't fully brace himself for the gravity of his actions. The setting sun cast long shadows across the forest, serving as a grim reminder of what he was about to do. Eventually, during the late hours of the night, he arrived at a desolate location where there was no one in sight.

Taking a deep breath, Basi stepped out of his car. As he opened the dicky, he steeled himself for the sight of Anwar's lifeless body. But what he found instead was unexpected – Anwar still breathing, his chest rising and falling rhythmically. Then Anwar opened his eyes, but he was immobile. He suffered significant blood loss, which prevented him from moving his muscles.

Basi's heart skipped a beat. He had never expected to find Anwar alive. Confusion and doubt clouded his mind. what should he do next?

He realised that Anwar was in a condition of suspended animation, which is the temporary (short- or long-term) slowing or stopping of biological function in order to preserve physiological capacities, which was the reason Linsha was unable to take Anwar's pulse. She believed Anwar had passed away at that same moment because of this.

As Basi pondered his next move, the weight of the situation settled upon him. Anwar might be alive, but he posed a constant threat to Linsha's well-being. The thought of her suffering clenched Basi's fists, fueling a fire within him.

Reluctantly, Basi made a difficult decision. If Anwar lived, Linsha would never find peace. Basi believed that sometimes, sacrifices had to be made for the greater good. And so, with a heavy heart, he gently maneuvered Anwar into the driver's seat.

A great load that he knew would eternally cast a shadow over his conscience was bearing down on him in the form of the decision's weight. Even someone as evil as Anwar, the idea of taking their lives made him question his morality. But Basi prepared himself to make the extreme decisions that fate seemed to require in order to protect his sister from the grasps of imminent danger.

Basi closed his eyes briefly, summoning the strength to carry out his plan. Anwar's foot was put on the accelerator pedal by him.The vehicle sped off. After colliding with a large branch of a tree. Anwar's skull had a terrifying explosion-like impact as a result of the accident, which was so severe that it left a scene of complete destruction. At the same time, the collision's force compressed his upper torso in an uncomfortable fashion. The cumulative effect of these horrific occurrences formed a vivid and unsettling picture of the incident's seriousness.

Dr. Arnab's perplexity over the recorded time of death in the autopsy report unveils a complex web of events that took place surrounding the demise of Anwar. Initially, both Dr. Arnab and Ankhitha were resolute in their conviction that Anwar had met his tragic end on July 19, 2020, a consequence of the brutal act inflicted upon him by Linsha's forceful wielding of a rod. This belief was grounded in their assessment of the available evidence and their judgments, cementing this timeframe as a factual cornerstone in their understanding of the case.

But in actuality, he didn't pass away then since on July 20, 2020, Basi murdered Anwar. The death occurred at the precise time

The mere mention of "divorce" in India, a nation where social status is highly valued, has huge ramifications that go well beyond the immediate couple concerned. Due to this cultural setting, many Indian parents prioritise their social status above all else, which frequently causes them to believe that getting a divorce could harm the reputation of their entire family. Couples like Linsha must manage a difficult web of demands caused by the weight of tradition, parental expectations, and community perceptions.

The tragic tale of Linsha demonstrates how these cultural expectations can have a profoundly negative effect on people's lives. Despite her sincere desire for her parents' love and support during a trying time, their engrained concern over sullying the family name trumped her emotional wellbeing. This demonstrates the dramatic contrast between the traditional focus on maintaining appearances and the contemporary urge for empathy and empowerment.

Killing Anwar was an act of desperation for Basi, because he believed there was no other option. Guilt etched deep into his soul as he stood over the lifeless body of Linsha's husband. It was not a decision he had made lightly, but one borne out of a desperate need to protect his sister from the torment she had endured for far too long.

Anwar, a man once welcomed into their family with open arms, had become a monster behind closed doors. His charming facade crumbled away, revealing a dark and twisted side that Linsha had become the unfortunate target of.

In the midst of his turmoil, a soft whimper drew his attention. Linsha emerged from the shadows, her eyes filled with a mixture of relief and sorrow. Basi's heart shattered as he realized the burden he had carried was not his alone. Linsha too had suffered from the weight of their secret.

Tears streamed down Basi's face as he embraced his sister, their shared pain merging into a single bond. They were victims of a broken system, trapped in a world that offered no solace. But in that dark moment, they found strength in each other's arms.

Together, they made a vow to protect one another, to navigate the aftermath of their actions side by side. They knew that justice might elude them, but their love and resilience would guide them forward. The path of redemption stretched before them, fraught with challenges, yet illuminated by a newfound hope.

When seen through the eyes of the outside world, Basi and Linsha can appear to be people with an attitude of arrogance and self-centeredness. Others can easily mistake their assured demeanour and seeming total focus on their own interests for being cold or disconnected. Yet underneath this apparent façade, a nuanced emotional tapestry often goes unnoticed by outsiders.

A sea of misery that is deep within of them, arising from events they have had but rarely talk about, ebbs and flows. Even though they were hidden, these encounters left a lasting impression on their souls. There are pockets of intense sadness that cast shadows over their thoughts amid the appearances of outward self-assurance. These grief may be caused by individual losses, dashed hopes, or the weight of unspoken obligations individuals bear.

In addition, they continue to harbour a complex emotion called guilt that silently undermines their sense of self. They may feel guilty about earlier choices they made or deeds they wish they could take back. As a continual reminder of their frailty, it forces people to conduct their lives cautiously and reflectively.

The arrogant persona they project is actually just a coping mechanism they've created to hide their vulnerabilities from an often cruel world. Their internal conflict serves as a reminder that they are all human and that our shared emotional landscapes are frequently more complex than our outward appearances. Basi and Linsha are complex people who defy easy classification because of their journey, which comprises the battle to balance the masks they put on with the sincerity of their buried pain. They will always have to deal with it. They must continue to keep THE SECRETS BEHIND THE DOORWAY - forever.

www.ingramcontent.com/pod-product-compliance
Lightning Source LLC
LaVergne TN
LVHW041027150826
845672LV00001B/227

* 9 7 9 8 8 9 1 8 6 1 2 2 0 *